ROYALIST
— ON THE —
RUN

JOHN GILBERT

authorHOUSE®

AuthorHouse™
1663 Liberty Drive
Bloomington, IN 47403
www.authorhouse.com
Phone: 1-800-839-8640

Published by AuthorHouse   04/27/2012

ISBN: 978-1-4685-0432-3 (sc)
ISBN: 978-1-4685-0433-0 (e)

Any people depicted in stock imagery provided by Thinkstock are models, and such images are being used for illustrative purposes only.
Certain stock imagery © Thinkstock.

This book is printed on acid-free paper.

CONTENTS

ROYALIST

— ON THE —

RUN

A Solomon Hawke adventure

Prologue

S olomon Hawke is the son of a wealthy, landowner who is a strong supporter of King Charles 1.

In 1643 at the start of the civil war Solomon is sent north from Oxford to escape a deadly rival and his adventures include fighting for a Scottish nobleman and a Barbary Corsair.

The first book follows his efforts to survive fighting on the losing side and at the same time trying to rescue his family from the wrath of Cromwell.

Solomon is a strong and well educated, if rather naïve, young man when he goes to Scotland at the age of 18. Despite being a dying military practice, his skill as an archer often comes in handy and he soon becomes well versed in the arts associated with modern military matters, politics and romance.

Chapter One

THE INCIDENT
(July 1643)

It was a fair fight on my part, no one ever suggested anything else but the result led me to being sent north to Montrose and his Royalist army and my first battle. It was the day of the annual feast where my father invited workers to a picnic and an afternoon of games followed by a grand ball in the evening for local landowners. Despite the confused political and social chaos of the time, my father was determined to retain some normality although this was becoming increasingly difficult.

The civil war that had divided the country into the two warring factions had now spread to all parts of the country and Oxfordshire was no exception. Our county was generally in favour of the King and my family were fully committed to his cause with my two brothers being officers in the Royalist army and my father being a strong political ally to the crown.

The feast was a brief, pleasant interlude in these frighteningly turbulent times.

Knowing many of the farm labourers, thatchers, shepherds and cowmen, my brothers and I had in the past hung around the edges of the picnic and joined in some of the games with local children. Tables of pies, bread, cheese, fruits and sweets were set out by the labourers' wives who were dressed in their Sunday attire and a cask of ale was being distributed to the men.

My eldest brother Tom wandered over with a tankard of ale.

'No beer for you Sol,' he shouted with laughter in his voice and continuing to treat me as the youngster rather than my real age of eighteen. He and Ben, the middle of us three brothers, were well past youngster's games but they sometimes joined in the men's wrestling, throwing and archery competitions. Tom's strength of personality as well as his obvious physical strength had made him into a renowned soldier and a popular leader of men. He had, from an early age, practiced soldier's skills and for years we had trained together and I sensed a wager was about to materialise. I was right.

'What about the archery competition Sol? I fancy your chances but I will give you a run for your money. A shilling says I get through more rounds than you.'

To look at us it was fairly obvious that Tom and I were brothers and our father's sons. We were both over six feet tall, broad shouldered and blond whereas Ben was a slim six feet tall with black wavy hair. This and his dark eyes always reminded us of our greatly missed mother who had died two years previously from an illness that had ravaged our village. Having spent much time administering to the workers who had also become infected, she eventually also succumbed to the pestilence.

Tom knew that archery was my real strength and it was just like him to encourage me to do something at which I might have a chance of some success. After giving me a hearty smack on the back he led me across to where the archery was being organised. Most of the men involved were young farmhands and gamekeepers but I was surprised to see three well-dressed young men also close to the arena.

'Hello there Thomas,' said one of the men greeting my brother.

'Good afternoon Nicholas, let me introduce you to my brother Solomon; Solomon this is Nicholas Caxton, Edward Key and Henry Wood, they are lieutenants who have served with me in Prince Rupert's army.'

I greeted them but wondered about the stiffness of attitude, of my usually ebullient brother, towards Nicholas Caxton.

'Thought I would show these yokels what a good archer looks like Thomas, are you shooting?'

'I intend to Nicholas, along with young Solomon.'

'What about a wager Thomas?'

'Now if this was musket or sword I might take up the wager but against you Nicholas I would just be wasting a shilling, I have seen you shoot before, but I might suggest a challenge from young Solomon here who is certainly a better shot than me.'

'Boy against man seems hardly fair but I will give you good odds, say a pound to a shilling as to who gets further.'

I was shocked at Tom's speed of acceptance on my behalf and presumed, without saying anything that he was betting with his own money.

We all three eventually entered the competition and shot in pairs against the farm workers whose archery skills varied greatly. By the time the competition was down to the last four, Tom had been knocked out by Luke Fox, our aptly named gamekeeper. I drew Luke in the next round but before our turn we watched Nicholas Caxton ease through to the final with a devastating five centre shots out of six. Luke and I had a close fight but I won with one more centre shot than him.

'Good luck in the final Solomon,' said Luke 'I must say I have no great affection for our esteemed lieutenant, even if he is a talented soldier, having seen the way he treated my sister Mary.'

I was about to ask what had happened when the competition organiser called Caxton and myself to the firing place.

'Come on Solomon Hawke, let's get this over and done with so I can collect my winnings,' said Caxton in a very haughty and offhand manner.

I must admit he was the best-dressed man I had seen other than Prince Rupert. He wore his leather doublet over a fine white shirt, fashionable baggy breeches and a colourfully ribboned sash around his middle. His friends held his sword and feathered hat while he shot his first set of arrows.

We had six arrows each, shot in two sets of three. After the first round we both had full marks. In the second round Caxton had two centres and one outer. On taking my last round Caxton whispered as he passed me: 'I hope you know what's good for you boy, I don't expect to lose to you.'

I was totally shocked by this and my first shot hit the outer. I heard chuckles from Caxton and his friends, which made me angry. Tom had always told me when we practiced swordplay that it's fine to be angry but always keep aware of your state of mind. I knew I had to channel my anger into my shooting and I powered two arrows into the centre in double quick time. This brought a spontaneous round of applause from the onlookers and I turned to see Caxton glaring straight at me.

'Three extra arrows each from an increased distance will decide the winner, Solomon to shoot first,' said the organiser. My strength as an archer is accuracy from long distance and I hit two centres and one outer at the distance close to 200 yards. Caxton looked uncomfortable hitting an outer with his first and missing the target altogether with his second. He threw down his bow and marched off shouting to his friends to pay me the pound. For a few moments everyone silently watched this petulant display before a rather uneasy chatter started as people moved away from the scene.

'Looks like you've made a friend,' said Tom who had collected the winnings. 'He is worth watching and I don't trust him after his involvement in some unpleasant behaviour after the battle at Edgehill. Anyway let's enjoy the rest of the day; I will see you later at the ball.'

'Great shooting Solomon,' said Luke who had wandered over after the final. 'Caxton seems to rile anyone he meets and as I said he was certainly not a gentleman where Mary is concerned. Still, he has been warned to keep away from her.'

When the afternoon activities had finished I returned to the house just as three riders were leaving. My father standing at the front door recognised my questioning expression.

'Messengers from Prince Rupert have reported a victory by Lord Wilmot and his cavalry at Roundaway Down; let's pray the end will come soon.'

Despite the good news I could see the sadness in my father's face but he suddenly looked up with a smile and said 'I hear you did well in the archery today Solomon, well done. Will I see you at the ball tonight?'

I assured him I would attend and went to my room where I was finding it difficult to get Caxton's words out of my thoughts until a knock on the door made me sit up with a jolt. My brother Ben entered with a parcel.

'Thought you would like this' he said as he handed the parcel which turned out to be a play 'The White Devil' by John Webster.

Ben was very much a literary man and although he had proved his worth in the cavalry I knew he was inwardly devastated by the confrontational situation we all found ourselves in unlike Tom who seemed to thrive on it.

'It's a good read but a pity we cannot see the play performed, I hope you enjoy it. Did Tom tell you we are off tomorrow to meet Prince Rupert at Bristol?'

I replied that indeed I did sadly know they were to take the troop to support the main army and we hugged each other in a spontaneous sign of affection.

'We will be fine Sol, Prince Rupert is a fine leader and our losses have been small compared to the Parliamentarians,' he said with a slightly less than confident note to his voice.

He left and I changed for the ball.

It was a fine occasion, considering the circumstances, although not as lavish as before the war. I ate from the buffet and mingled with some of the landowners and their sons. Ladies in their finery chatted together and a little dancing took place as the evening wore on. As it was a warm and humid evening I strolled outside for some fresh air and I rounded the back of the house where I could see servants working in the kitchen. It was dark but enough light came from the house for me to see what looked like a scuffle taking place under the trees. A scream made me run over just in time to see Caxton punching a girl in the face.

'You bitch,' he shouted, 'no-one refuses me.'

I caught his arm as he was about to repeat the punch and pushed him to the ground. The girl backed away and as I turned towards her Caxton hit me with a large branch he had picked off the floor. I went down but I managed to jump up quickly to face him.

'How dare you attack me you bastard, clear off before I teach you a lesson you will not forget.'

I moved over towards the girl who was sorting out her clothing and sobbing snottily.

'Let's go.' I said to her and took her arm.

'Leave her boy,' said Caxton who then spun me around and struck me in the face.

I quickly picked myself up and charged him with my head into his stomach. He was stronger and inches taller than me and remembering Tom's lessons I hit him hard before he could regain his breath. I turned away from him but I turned back on hearing the scrape of a drawn sword. I was unarmed and stood no chance and the sight of Caxton suddenly being tackled to the floor from the side was a complete surprise. Tom dragged Caxton to his feet and punched him hard in the stomach. Disarmed and winded Caxton was kneeling on the floor when a number of people emerged from the kitchens.

They could see us but would not have known what happened and Tom told Caxton to crawl back to his lodgings. He left muttering curses and threats.

Chapter Two

THE JOURNEY
(July 1643–January 1644)

T he four horses were already saddled with saddlebags packed when Tom, Ben and my father came out to see us off.

'Take the route I explained to you last night Solomon but take care and be prepared to travel at night,' my father suggested. Then with a genuine hug of affection he wished me good luck. My brothers were obviously affected by the moment and Tom told Luke to try and keep me out of trouble. We parted with rather strained smiles and trotted off down the road.

After around three hours of virtually silent riding we came across a troop of cavalry, which luckily was being led by one of Tom's close friends. Having asked what we doing and giving us advice about what to expect they allowed us to proceed without having to read the papers of authority which my father had endorsed. After another couple of hours we watered our horses in a stream and lay on the grass while our mounts rested.

'I expect Tom explained to you why we left so quickly Luke,' who with a mouth full of bread just nodded.

Luke had been about to leave with Tom and his cavalry troop but as soon as the situation had been explained to him he was only too pleased to accompany me. Luke and I had been friends for as long as I could remember despite the difference in upbringing and we spent many exciting hours together hunting deer and fowl. He was not as tall as me but was extremely strong and he had learnt his gamekeeping and hunting skills from his father who was reputed to be the best poacher in the county. My father had saved Luke's father from the fierce arm of the law by making him his gamekeeper and Luke recognised the help my father had provided his family by stating his loyalty in return.

The evening before we left was a fraught one. Tom had explained what had happened with Caxton to my father and emphasised that this politically powerful and vindictive man was likely to try and gain his revenge and he thought it best if I was removed from the scene as soon as possible.

'Son, I want you to travel to Lathom House in the morning and stay there until I send you instructions. The Earl of Derby will be pleased to see you again as will his wife who, if my memory serves me well, treated you like a long lost son during out last visit.'

I had made this journey to Lancashire before and I remembered it took about ten days of sensible riding. My father however had given me a map of places to visit or avoid on the way which was likely to make the journey a few days longer.

'How was Mary when you left?'

'Shocked and upset, but I calmed her and my father down and warned my brothers to avoid Caxton. She will stay with my uncle's family for a while until Caxton is out of the picture. She told me to thank you again for your help and hoped you would not get into any trouble because of the assistance you had given her. I said I would look after you and she laughed, although she knew that we would not see each other for some time.'

'We should move on, I hoped we could reach Stow before nightfall.'

Like most people travelling in these dangerous times we were well armed although we were not lavishly dressed. Both of us wore leather jerkins and caps and we looked more like farmhands than an eighteen year old landowner's son and his escort. Luke had his fowling piece slung over his shoulder and I had a sword and pistol at my side. My spare horse carried my bow, quiver, extra arrows along with clothes and a tent. Luke was in charge of the main supply of food although we expected to be able to buy food along the way. The weather was good and we enjoyed the freedom of the first part of the journey.

In Stow we lodged at an inn where we were well looked after once the owner had collected the price of a night with food. There were other obvious Royalists in the inn along with others less obvious. Working out friend from foe was one of the main problems of the day but there was a relatively friendly and relaxed attitude amongst the locals and once they heard where we came from we were made welcome. After some wholesome hot food we spent time talking to two cavalrymen who warned us that a number of small bands of Parliamentarians had raided farms a few miles to the north. Although this was worrying, the men felt these were just reconnaissance raids, which were trying to determine the level of support there was for their cause and presumed they would rapidly retreat with any information they had gained.

The next day we followed the road for a while and then move to the edge of the woodlands that covered the higher ground. We felt we would be more able to spot any riders before they saw us from this advantageous position. By the middle of the day we came across a wood, which stretched across our route and decided to pass through it on the relatively clear though narrow route where others had passed before. After about a mile we decided it was time for a rest. Luke suggested I go a little further until there was some decent grass for the horses, as he wanted to relieve himself. He dismounted, tied up his horses and went off into the trees. I moved down the narrow track hoping to find a suitable area to stop and must have ridden for about half a mile when suddenly two men jumped out in front of me. One held a musket and the other a fowling piece. I stopped and a voice behind me ordered me to get down.

'Get him off the track. Move you scum,' the obvious leader ordered.

With a musket pressed against my spine I was pushed deeper into the wood with another man leading my horses. The leader armed with a pistol walked to the side of me and after about twenty minutes we came across a clearing with a hut at one edge.

'Take the horses behind the hut Dan,' said the leader, 'and bring in the baggage.'

I was taken into the hut and roughly pushed into a chair and tied up.

'Well now Isaac what have we got here? Looks like a lost little rich boy by the quality of his horses.'

'We should get a good price for them to be sure Tobias. Let's strip off these fine clothes; I could do with a good pair of boots.'

There was suddenly a crash from the back of the hut.

'Sounds if young Dan is having trouble with the horses go and give him a hand.'

Isaac left the hut and Tobias stood covering me with his pistol. After a couple of minutes there was a knock at the door.

'Get in here you fools.'

Tobias impatiently went to the door until he was about a foot away from it when it suddenly burst open smashing into Tobias who fell backwards sending me and my chair hurtling across the room. I struggled to my feet and kicked the pistol out of Tobias hand, which went off with a deafening crash in the corner of the room. Tobias jumped up in front of me and with my arms pinned to the chair I head butted him across his nose. He went down wailing, I went down dazed and bloody.

'And I thought you were a gentleman!' said Luke who was standing in the door holding his firearm.

'Who taught you to fight like that?'

'Well it's not often you practice fighting while tied to a chair is it. Other than talking him to death I couldn't think of anything else at the time,' I responded rather testily.

Luke untied me and I tied Tobias up with the same rope.

'What shall we do with the other two?' I asked.

'They won't bother us.' Luke said rather darkly.

I went outside to a water butt to clean the blood off my face and saw Luke's work. Dan was tied to a tree and unconscious, Isaac was face down in the mud obviously in a far worse state and when I turned him over could see his throat was cut from ear to ear, I stopped in my tracks and threw up near to the water butt.

'I had no choice, if he had given a warning I didn't know what the man in the hut would do,' said Luke.

'You saved my life that is certain, thanks, now let's get out of here, we don't know if there are only three of them,' I said shakily.

'What shall we do with the other two?' said Luke as we re-entered the hut.

Tobias joined in the conversation as soon as he heard this.

'So you have killed that idiot Isaac then, no loss there. But what have you done with Dan my brother?'

'Tied to a tree with a bad headache,' said Luke.

'Let me loose, let me help him; I know when I'm beaten. I'm no danger to you now.'

Luke looked threateningly towards him but I had decided to release him and said so.

We collected our packs and horses, took all the firearms we could find and tied Tobias by the waist to Dan's tree. He would be able to get free in a few minutes by which time we had ridden away from the scene.

'What do you think Luke, just bandits or deserters?'

'Probably both,' he replied.

Over the next three days we travelled carefully and therefore quite slowly.

Travelling at night was difficult, whereas during daytime at least we could see most of the likely problem areas.

We eventually came to a destination suggested by my father; the estate of Geoffrey Gill. I had been here once before some years ago and remembered the general layout of his land.

The house stood in the centre of a large parkland area with a number of scattered wooded areas. From our woodland outlook we could see activity around the house, which seemed military in style. Some riders left the house and their attire suggested a Royalist cavalry detachment although we realised we must be certain of the house's allegiance before we approached it. Hanging back in the trees we tethered our four horses and munched on some bread and cheese we had bought at a nearby village where we had also gained some information about the local area.

The political situation in this part of the West Midlands was unstable and confused. Some towns were Royalist strongholds but many villages were starting to show allegiance to the Parliamentarians, especially since a number of Royalist press gang raids had taken place robbing the farms of the men while further north it was said that Nantwich had sided with the Parliamentarians.

After a cold but dry night the house looked quiet enough for us to ride down and make ourselves known to Geoffrey Gill the owner and a past business acquaintance of my father's. On entering the grounds of the house we were confronted by guards. The leader asked who we were and what we were about in a distinctly foreign accent.

'I am Captain Marco Lopez, commander of Sir Geoffrey Gills guard. I will take you to him,' he said whereupon he ordered his men to disarm us and take the horses to the stables. He and one guard took us into the entrance hall of the house and a message was sent to Sir Geoffrey. He arrived in a flourish of fine clothes covering a grossly overweight body followed by two more guards.

'Who have we here then Captain?'

'I am Solomon Hawke Sir and this is my escort Luke Fox,' I interrupted. 'My father suggested I might seek refuge here for a night on my travels north.' I perceived a look of frustration on Sir Geoffrey's face and continued, 'if this is not possible we would be grateful for a little food and a chance for our horses to rest until the evening.' Sir Geoffrey put on a rather false smile and gestured for us to sit down.

'Solomon it is good to see you after such a long time, you are welcome to stay the night although you must realise that the Parliamentarians have begun to take a stronger hold in this area and you could be in more danger if you remained here for too long. You may use the stable lads' bunkroom near the stables and I will make sure food is sent to you. If you are still here in the evening we will dine together.'

The Captain escorted us out to the stables where we untacked our horses and moved our bags to the very basic bunkroom. After a few moments a knock on the door revealed a man carrying some food and beer. Behind him stood the Captain who suggested that we join him on one of the benches outside.

'You are Spanish Captain?'

'I am,' he replied.

'Why would a Spanish Captain be fighting in this mess?' asked Luke.

'I am a mercenary and fight for whoever pays me. However I agree with you this war is a mess. People do not seem to know who they support and many who have made up their minds are not certain why.

Conflicts I have been involved with in the past seemed to divide people easily. Here even families are divided. I can understand those with puritanical zeal following the Parliamentarians but even the Royalists follow the same religion if rather less fervently. I have been recruited by Prince Rupert and have recently arrived in your cold, wet country. The only advantages I can see of living here are the urm . . ., well that aside what is your story if I may ask?' he said trying to brush past his personal likes.

I explained that we were travelling to a friend's house to the north and he responded by hoping we managed to get there without too much difficulty.

'A Spanish Captain with his looks,' said Luke later when we had gone back into the stables to groom our horses, 'fairly obvious what he likes about this country and probably any other for that matter.' I must have looked rather nonplussed because Luke continued;

'Women, Solomon and lots of them I expect, along with the money he can earn.'

I nodded in agreement.

'Well he has something in common with you then Luke.'

'What a love of women and money?'

'No it's in his name, you're the Fox he's the Wolf. Lopez is Spanish for wolf.'

'That's three things we have in common then,' Luke laughed.

We spent the afternoon in the stable area as we were asked not to wander outside. It was just turning dusk when four armed guards pushed their way into our room and dragged us roughly into the house where Sir Geoffrey and the Captain were sitting.

'My apologies young men,' said Sir Geoffrey rather disdainfully 'but our situation has changed. I have never been a staunch Royalist and I have sent a message to the Parliamentarians which states that I and my household are fully on their side in the conflict. You two, on the other hand, are now prisoners of the cause and will be handed over to a force that should reach us in the morning. Take them to the lock up.'

I could not think of anything to say although Luke found some appropriate earthy comments, which I mentally fully endorsed. On looking at the two seated men I noticed the Captain just looking straight at me with a face like stone while Sir Geoffrey seemed to be gloating over his capture which was probably going to help him with his new

Roundhead friends. We were bundled into a
solid locked room at the back of the house
and we could hear the guards outside chatting
about their change of allegiance. They did not
seem too concerned as either way they were
being paid by Sir Geoffrey.

'Christ what are we going to do now?'
blasphemed Luke in a way which showed
that his upbringing was rather less than
puritanical.

'No idea, but we must try to get away from
here before the Roundheads arrive. I must
say I am more surprised about the Captain
than Sir Geoffrey whom even my father was
rather dubious about.'

We scratched about in the dark room
trying to find some way out but the room was
completely empty and had no windows and
just one door. We could find nothing to use as
a weapon and no alternative way out. Later in
the night, unable to sleep, we heard the voice
of the Captain talking to the guards. It turned
out he had brought them some wine from the
house and told two of them to go and rest in
the stables while he and the remaining two
men would stay on guard. After a short while
we heard what sounded like a scuffle outside
which ended with the door opening and the
Captain greeting us with: 'Come on you two

let's get out of this rat trap.' I blinked in the light of the lamp he was holding and nearly tripped over one of the prone guards.

'What's going on?' said Luke 'I thought you were on the fat man's side.'

'I am not in the habit of letting other people select which side I play for, in any case I have given my word to Prince Rupert and a Lopez does not go back on his word now, if you don't mind, we will relieve the other two guards of their duty, collect the horses and get out of here.'

It was not difficult to disarm the remaining guards as they were completely surprised by our armed entrance and we took them outside and tied them to a gate.

'Before we go I think I would like to leave Sir Geoffrey with something to remember me by,' said Lopez who strode up to the house while we collected six horses and let the others out into the field.

On arriving at the front of the house we could see flames were already consuming the main room to the left of the door as Lopez ran out, he theatrically mounted his horse and after waving his hat at the house cantered off down the drive. Luke and I took one look at each other burst into laughter and charged off down the road after him.

We soon moved away from the main road and travelled along the edges of woods trying to avoid lights from houses and camps. We managed to ride until dawn without any hindrance before stopping to rest ourselves and the horses. We pushed our way deep into a thickly wooded area and found an area with some grass for grazing where we hobbled the horses and sat down on our blankets. It had been a cold night but I only noticed the chill in the air after I had sat down.

'Not much like Spain then?' said Luke

'It gets as cold as a rock on many nights where I come from but in the day at least we see and can feel the Sun. Now we have to decide our next move.'

'How did you get mixed up with Gill, Captain?' I asked.

'I was sent by Prince Rupert to link up with Lord Byron who is now the Field-Marshal in this area. He has a number of Spanish mercenaries and I was to be assigned to them. I was told to stop off at Sir Geoffrey's on the way and try to gain some information about support in this area. Prince Rupert had warned me that Sir Geoffrey was unreliable but in my role as a mercenary he thought I would be easily swayed by his money. Many men have changed sides in this conflict so I hear, some immediately after being on the losing side in a battle. Sir Geoffrey has now found out that I am not one of them.'

'We should move on this afternoon and find a farm or village where we can gather some information. I saw a track leading from the wood just before this thicket which hopefully leads to a farm or woodman's cottage.'

The Captain was right. We found a cottage at the edge of the wood where a frightened and wary family were hiding in their wood store. They only came out after one of the children started to cough repeatedly and only then very cautiously.

Luke spoke to them first and his manner seemed to calm them although the site of our more exotic Captain in his chest armour and helmet made them back off in fear. After a few more calming words the family came out and we sat around the front of the cottage and listened to their tales of movement of men and horses. It seemed that this area was strongly Royalist and the woodsman was a King's forester. The main news was that Nantwich to the north had declared support for the Parliamentarians and Lord Byron was now moving towards the town and cutting off any supplies while setting up his command post at Acton, a nearby village. The forester gave us directions and we now moved more confidently down the minor roads towards Acton, which would be about a day's ride. We were challenged five times by Royalist Cavalry but were allowed to pass due to Lopez's documents signed by The Prince.

On arrival at Acton in the evening the camp adjutant read our documents and assigned us some tented accommodation. He said he would take our letters to Lord Byron.

We were summoned to the camp commandant's residence later that evening. Lord Byron had taken over the largest tavern in the village for his staff and it was obvious on entering that they were pleased with the arrangement. A number of officers were dining and drinking while being served by some seemingly very excitable women.

'This is more like it. You know I didn't come to this damp and depressing country just to sleep in woods or in a tent with ruffians like you two,' Lopez said with a big grin crossing his handsome, tanned face.

An officer approached us from another room and we were ushered in, to be immediately addressed by Lord Byron.

'I am pleased to see you Captain, my Spanish contingent has done me proud but lacks a leader of your experience. Captain Clarke will show you to your quarters later and set out your orders. Now what do we have here, young Solomon Hawke and escort? I have read your letter of introduction and I know and respect your father greatly Solomon I will therefore try to help you reach your destination although this might be difficult and take some time as Cheshire and Lancashire are posing a few problems we still need to overcome. In the mean time I hope you will be satisfied with your tented quarters and you may come to the tavern as Captain Lopez's 'officer guests' whenever he wishes. I will send you some instructions in the next few days but I would ask you not to leave the village until we can be surer of your safety.'

I thanked the Commander and Luke, Lopez and I left the room.

'A striking leader is he not?' said Captain Clarke. Now if you three would like to join the officers in the other room, they have been briefed as to who you are and would welcome you I am sure.'

We were made welcome and Lopez soon made his charms known to the women who cheerfully responded to the amorous attention he was giving them. Luke and I chatted with the officers, two of whom knew my brothers and stated nothing but praise for them. I must admit I was now more at ease than I had been for some time. The warm fire, the ale and the food relaxed me to such an extent that I could even cope with some of the women's teasing which on a normal occasion would have greatly embarrassed me.

'Leave the poor lad alone Betsy,' said one of the older women to the younger and very much prettier aforementioned.

At this point Luke whispered in my ear, 'you know these women want your money in exchange for a romp.'

I must have blushed because the women laughed and moved their attention to the other officers. I noticed Lopez being led away by the tall dark-headed Betsy who turned and winked at me as she left.

'I think we should call it a night Sol before we lose what little money we have even if afterwards we might have thought it money well spent.'

We staggered back to our tents and flopped on the wooden beds and wrapped our blankets around us to ward off the chill of the night. I slept soundly until I was woken by Luke who said there was food available and that we were to be issued with instructions once we had fed.

After our breakfast of porridge we walked over to the command tent via a large flat field where musketeers were practicing their firing drill. The officer in charge was issuing orders in a way that portrayed little confidence in the ability of the men.

'We will continue until everyone of you can fire at least two rounds a minute and I mean by rounds I mean balls not scouring sticks.'

'You use a rifle Luke and fire three rounds a minute, why are these so slow?'

'Practice Solomon,' said a voice in a Spanish accent,' although if they have not fired while being fired at, I doubt if they will manage more than one shot per minute.'

'Captain Lopez I presume you managed to fire off a few rounds yourself last night,' Luke quipped before we all walked over to watch the drill.

'They have the equipment with full bandoleers but in battle they must be disciplined to fire off a volley after half a minute. At short range a well drilled troop of men can cause some withering damage, but they must stand while being fired at which can only be achieved by a disciplined force who trust each other. My Spanish mercenaries will stand but will these peasants and peacocks? I am not so sure.'

On reaching the command tent we were greeted by Captain Clarke.

'Good morning gentlemen, I have your instructions from Lord Byron which amounts to the fact that the regiment will be moving north through Cheshire to Nantwich starting at dawn tomorrow. Lord Byron has said you may join the regiment and when a safe passage north is created you may go on your way. I suggest you travel with the baggage train where perhaps you can assist with the general transporting of all our trappings.'

'Thank you Captain we would be happy to do as you ask; please thank Lord Byron for his patronage.'

We returned to the tented area and started chatting to the men from the neighbouring tents. After the usual round of complaints about the food and the weather, which was now starting to turn cold with a few flurries of sleet mixed in with the drizzle, we found out more about the local political situation. We were being assigned to the regiment, which was to attempt to break the siege of Nantwich but before that, there was likely to be some stiff opposition in Cheshire along our route. The men seemed confident about their leaders and were pleased with the successes they had achieved up to now. The tent next to ours was occupied by three brothers named Garret who had volunteered after their father and his estate had suffered at the hand of the Parliamentarians. The father was now imprisoned in Nottingham while the rest of the family had been forced to flee to Oxford where they were being cared for by relatives. They were all tall, strong and friendly young men who quickly struck a friendship with Luke who was more than willing to show the men his rifled firearm, which as he was explaining is a more accurate weapon than their muskets if a little slower to load.

'I can still fire three rounds a minute,' said Luke but I must admit this is harder to do than with a musket.'

Leaving the group to their weaponry discussion I decided to have a walk around the camp. It was a well-organised area of tents and shelters with men practicing pike drills although I saw no sword activities taking place. The musket drills continued in the field and I watched the officers trying to improve the quality of the men's performance. Most of the men had the twelve steps it needs to fire a matchlock musket although some still could not get them in absolutely the correct order.

The officers would shout the sequence of 'Bite,' (the cartridge and the pan filled). 'Match;' (checked it is alight). 'Hold;' (the musket muzzle pointing upwards). 'Pour;' (the rest of powder poured into the barrel). 'Insert;' (the ball dropped into the barrel). 'Push;' (the cartridge paper wedged into barrel). 'Remove;' (the ramrod taken out and the wadding and ball pushed down the barrel). 'Replace;' (the ramrod). 'Blow;' (on match which is replaced into jaws). 'Open;' (the pan). 'Present;' (the musket to firing position). 'Aim and Fire.' When attempting this under the pressure of time a few went off with no ball in the barrel and one ramrod went flying across the field.

'Which of you idiots has managed to fire some of The King's precious equipment across his acres?' shouted the officer.

A young man from the centre of the groups replied. 'It was me Sir, sorry Sir.'

After a short pause and a threatening stare the officer said in a deep voice. 'How long would it take you to run over there and retrieve it Walters?'

'Only a minute sir,' came the shaky reply.

'Well, that is precisely what you have. Men get ready to proceed with your drill on my command. Walters you had better get moving unless you want to look like a sieve, now run.'

Walters dropped his firearm and ran as the men went through their drill. If he did not get back to the firing line before the men shot he would stand no chance with forty nine poorly aimed muskets shooting at the targets in the distance and him directly in the firing line. Quite a crowd had now gathered and other men who had been standing around started shouting encouragement to Walters who was certainly moving quickly.

'Bite, Match, Hold' Pour,' came the instructions just as Walters collected his scouring stick, turned and ran straight towards forty nine raised muskets.

'Present, Aim, Fire came the order and the muskets all went off in a crashing, smoky volley.

I and the other spectators had rushed forward to see what was going to happen and when the smoke cleared Walters could be seen face down in the dirt about 20 yards from the firing line. He did not move for a few moments and then much to everyone's relief he slowly stood up with a startled look on his face.

'Doubt if you will do that again in a hurry Walters,' barked the officer. 'Now get back in line and let's see who else might require special attention.' I stood watching them practice over the next hour and they definitely improved after the Walters incident.

Chapter Three

THE BAGGAGE TRAIN
(January 1644)

I t took a good three hours to get the regiment and all of the baggage train away and on to the road. Luke and I being assigned to the train followed the last cart. There was a cavalry troop well to our rear and we could see other riders at a distance along the flanks of our procession.

The road was narrow and rutted and on a number of occasions we had to lend a hand to carts, which had become stuck or had slid off the side of the road. We moved at a very slow pace but the work and the company made it an eventful journey. Along with carts containing weapons, powder, food and tents there were carts full of women, children and a few sick or injured soldiers. The women were boisterous and I was spotted by Lopez's tall, dark haired tavern acquaintance.

'It's Solomon isn't it?' she said as we marched alongside her cart. 'I'm Betsy; don't you remember me from the tavern?'

'I remember you Betsy,' I said rather bashfully but at the same time again noticing how attractive she was.

'May I come and visit you when we make camp Solomon; the Captain said I would like you?'

'Perhaps you could but I would not like to deprive the Captain of your company.'

'Don't worry about him Solomon; he'll be too busy with his Spanish troop to have any time for me or any of the other girls.'

'Looks as though you've made a friend,' said Luke, who had been chatting and playing with two young children in the cart in front.

'Be careful you don't make a Spanish enemy at the same time,' he joked.

For two days we ploughed on behind the regiment until on the morning of the third day a commotion at the front made the carts behind concertina to a halt. Riders from the rear galloped past and musket fire could clearly be heard taking place ahead of the regiment's column.

One of the injured soldiers in a nearby cart said he thought the skirmishers in front must have come across some opposition.

From our position it was difficult to see what was happening but the lieutenant in charge of our train came trotting back to our guards and told us we had run into a regiment of Parliamentarians who were barring our passage to Nantwich. We could see our cavalry moving off to the sides.

'Protecting the flanks,' said the injured soldier 'I expect the boys up front will be digging in.'

'We are to move the baggage train to the top of that small hill,' said the Lieutenant, 'it will be safer there.'

We pushed, pulled and hauled the carts up the slope to the top of the hill with the women helping and the wounded that could walk limping behind. Once on the top we could see the position of the opposing forces. To our north the Parliamentarians had partly dug themselves a trench and wall although they seemed to be still working on it. Our troops were doing the same just out of musket range. It seemed nothing would happen for a while until suddenly from a hidden ditch half way across the divide, a troop of Parliamentarians stood up and fired into the midst of the labouring soldiers. Many men went down screaming or dead.

Immediately afterwards a mass of Parliamentarians leapt out of their ditch and ran towards our men. Lord Byron at this point showed why he is an astute leader. He had obviously prepared himself for a possible trap and from behind the group of wounded soldiers five hundred musketeers all loaded and primed ran forward to the trench. They waited as the Parliamentarians ran to no more than fifty yards from the ditch and let loose a devastating volley. Men went down in heaps before they could return fire in any numbers. The men in the ditch then stood up and along with around one hundred pikemen charged the opposition.

The Parliamentarians could not get a volley organised and hand to hand fighting of a scale I hoped I would never witness again took place. Musketeers were using their firearms to bludgeon their way through the throng while some were using their short sword they called a tuck, to stab and slash. This was no organised battle and although our men were pushing back the Roundheads they did not try to push home what advantage they had and a retreat was called.

Both sides returned to their trenches leaving the land in between littered with dead and injured men. I could hear the shouts and cries of men in the field, which was now being joined by the sobs and wailing from the women, and children in the carts. After a short time a Captain from our trench stood up with a trooper holding a white flag. They approached the injured and I heard him shout, although I could not hear what he said I found out later he was asking for a truce to treat the wounded.

Suddenly two shots rang out and the two men went down. A howl of anguish arose from our ranks and then silence. Then the most astonishing occurrence took place. Two of our pikemen stood up and walked out across the divide. I heard orders being shouted but the two men took no notice.

'They are the Garret brothers,' said Luke, who had eyesight like a hawk, 'and the third brother was holding the flag.'

The boys stooped down over the two shot men then stood up and after looking at each other started ramming their pike into any dead or injured Parliamentarians lying on the ground. A shout of horror came from the Parliamentarians who as one jumped out of their trench. Some fired shots but none hit the boys who just stood there with their pikes held out in front. I heard some strong orders from our officers and could see most of the men reloading although many, myself included, could not take their eyes off the scene. The Parliamentarians in their dozens charged wildly and angrily at the boys whereas our men were now steadily moving in a line three deep towards them. The two boys went down fighting; they injured a number of the opposition who had now run well into range of our musketeers.

I heard the distinct 'Aim, Fire,' command and a massive volley smashed into the front group of soldiers. The next line moved forward a pace and sent another volley crashing into the men who, if they had not been hit were now realising the folly of their action. A third volley took men mostly in their backs, after which, both sides again retreating to their trenches.

Everyone's attention had been on the battleground and many of the rear guard had gone down to re-enforce the front line. A shout from Luke made me turn to see a troop of Parliamentarian cavalry charging down the road towards us. We had little defence and not much time.

'Get the children away Luke,' I shouted.

Luke grabbed the two children hauled them on to the front of his horse and after a quick look round towards me rode down the hill towards our troops below. I grabbed a pike and jumped onto a cart containing two injured soldiers. The cavalry arrived and blasted off their carbines into the throng of people around the carts. One of the soldiers next to me was fatally hit and I fended off the slash of another cavalryman's sword. The people were now all running down the hill. Two more riders charged towards me firing and one horse crashed into the wheel, which knocked me off the cart. The riders attacked the other injured soldier and then charged off. I could not run down the hill because of the cavalry but I thought if I could get to a thicket about fifty yards away I might be safe.

'Don't leave me Solomon, please don't leave me,' it was Betsy hiding under the cart.

'Quick, we must run to that wood, can you make it?'

'Just try and catch me.'

I grabbed my pack from the cart and we ran along a hedge to the wood. I thought we had reached it without being seen until I saw one rider looking in our direction before cantering along the hedge towards us. I didn't have time to sort my bow out from my baggage and we dodged behind a large tree by the side of the track. I picked up a heavy branch I found on the ground and waited. The rider came past us at a trot and I ran out and hit him in the face with the branch. He fell off with a crash close to Betsy who to my astonishment jumped up and stabbed him in the throat with a large knife. He died spluttering and grabbing the wound. Betsy collapsed back and seemed in a state of shock.

Neither of us moved for a few moments but on looking back to the baggage train it seemed no one had seen what had happened. The cavalry horse had disappeared into the wood and the rider had nothing of any use to us except his clothes. We dragged him into the wood and took off his jacket for Betsy to wear. We thought about his trousers but they would have been far too large.

'We must find somewhere to hide,' I said and Betsy followed me as, after picking up my pack, I started making tracks into the wood.

'We will have to stay in the wood for the night but we can't light a fire, someone might see the smoke.'

We found a large tree with a hollowed out side and after scraping away some dead twigs we squeezed inside. I gave Betsy my blanket and went back outside to find some branches to cover the entrance. As there were no leaves on the trees I piled on the branches as thickly as I could and the crawled back into our hiding place. We had very little room and I put my arm around Betsy's shoulder.

'Now don't start getting any ideas.'

I started to remove my arm.

'Don't be silly Solomon I was only joking, let's cuddle up and share the little warmth we have.'

I did not think I would sleep but I did until I awoke with a start by something scratching around outside our hollow, this also woke Betsy.

'It's OK, only a squirrel,' I said.

Dawn was just about arriving although a blanket of fog enveloped the wood. Everything seemed very still and virtually silent. I was almost afraid to move just in case someone was around, but after a short time I peered out through the branches and could see no further than a few yards but could hear nothing so hoped it was safe.

'Do you have any food Solomon?'

I retrieved a few biscuits from my baggage but my drinking flask was virtually empty. We ate 'the worst breakfast any young man has ever treated me to,' according to Betsy whose ability to make fun out of dire situations continued to catch me out. We shared a quiet chuckle but soon realised we must move on.

After crawling out of the tree and stretching our cold and cramped bodies we walked to the edge of the wood. The fog had lifted enough for us to see that soldiers were down in the area where we had left the baggage train so we turned and started walking back through the wood.

About two hours later we came to a woodman's dilapidated hut, which at least had a water butt. The water was just about drinkable and I filled my flask from which we both drank a swallow. We moved on in silence and eventually came to the edge of the wood from where we could see a wide valley and a river meandering through it. There were no signs of life and we decided to go down to the river where hopefully the water might be cleaner than the contents of our flask. It took us an hour to reach the river although some of the land around it was almost waterlogged and we found the river itself to be flowing extremely quickly. We followed the course by walking along the natural bank, which was higher than the surrounding fields but became concerned that we were far too visible for this to be our best course of action in daylight.

In the distance a town had become visible while in the foreground there was a bridge crossing the river. We decided to go to the settlement, although we realised this might spell danger we needed food and shelter soon. We walked towards the bridge but had to jump into a drainage ditch when a troop of cavalry came riding down the road. They passed without incident and on reaching the bridge we hid underneath, between the walls and the very high level of the river. From our hideaway we could clearly survey the river and the valley although the road that crossed the river bridge was obscured from view. Around a hundred yards downstream was a small hut with a rowing boat on the bank next to it.

'I think we should wait until dark before we move any further,' I said and Betsy although obviously cold and hungry agreed. The days being short at this time of the year meant we did not have to wait long before it became dark enough for us to slink off down the side of the river to the uninhabited hut.

'Let's take the boat past the town,' said Betsy.

'Good idea, but we must find some food.'

'Leave that to me, if we can get into the town I know I can get food and will be less likely to get into trouble than you.'

We managed to get the boat, with oars from the hut, into the water and with a bit less than expert boatmanship we climbed into the craft and drifted downstream. On approaching the town we were swept under one bridge rather scarily but no one spotted us. We went past a wharf and managed to pilot the boat under the beams of a jetty.

'Take care Betsy,' I said as she climbed onto the jetty.

'If you are not back in an hour I am coming to look for you.'

'No don't, you will never find me, if I get into trouble and am not back just before dawn carry on down the river.'

With that last statement I started to realise that I was not used to being given instructions by a woman but Betsy seemed different to any woman I had met before. She seemed confident in the company of men but also a quick and decisive decision maker. I waited for what seemed half the night when I heard a shuffling of feet on the jetty. It was Betsy who scrambled down into the boat.

'Let's get out of here before all hell let's lose.'

I untied the boat, grabbed the oars and spun the boat out into the river. I aimed for the far bank where the current was strong and we flashed under a bridge which I only just saw in time and with the water so high, we had to duck our heads to avoid being crowned.

The river was getting wider and the plain either side was now broad and uninhabited and, although keeping the boat bow forward was sometimes a problem, we moved unmolested and unseen for miles.

In the middle of the afternoon we noticed the flow of the river was easing and we both voiced the same thought that we were close to the coastal estuary and the river would now become tidal. This boat was certainly not seaworthy so at a convenient bank we pulled in and due to the now very slow flow, were able to moor and climb out. We dragged the boat partly up the bank and looked around for a route out of the marshland that surrounded us.

In the distance a group of huts with smoke rising from them could be seen so with much effort we pulled the boat over the bank down into the marshland waterway amongst the reeds. We had to row and punt the boat through the dense vegetation, which was so high that we had difficulty aiming the boat towards the village. Having done this for an hour or so we collapsed exhausted into the bottom of the boat where we drank and ate some of the provisions Betsy had purloined from Nantwich.

Suddenly a voice barked.

'Don't move we have you covered.'

Looking up we were surrounded by men in what looked like flat-bottomed punts brandishing all kinds of weapons.

The men hauled us out of our boat and unceremoniously dumped us into a punt, which the men manoeuvred surprisingly quickly through the marsh. We arrived at the island, which contained the huts we had seen in the distance and were escorted up to the small village. We were told to sit on a bench outside one of the huts whereupon one of the men having been through my pack asked us what we were doing in the marsh.

'Betsy and I were caught up in a skirmish near to Nantwich and our only escape route was by river. We didn't know where the river went and finished up here in the marsh.'

'Just look at them Arthur,' said a woman who was at the front of the crowd watching us, 'they're cold and starving I shouldn't wonder, so stop interrogating them like you're the law and show them some hospitality.'

'Just trying to find out if they are a danger to us Martha, but I agree at the moment they can't do us any harm so take them inside and sort them out if you would.'

We went inside a surprisingly tidy and spacious room where we were soon given some soup and fish, both of which were delicious and much appreciated. Betsy was given some dry clothes and clean water to wash with. The room was warm if rather smoky and we gradually regained enough strength to tell Martha and the others in the hut, which included children who we were.

'My name is Solomon and this is Betsy,' I volunteered, 'and we would like to thank you for your kindness.'

'You are welcome, we don't get many visitors here and in these troubled times we are quite pleased about that. My husband was only trying to work out if you were a threat to us but we are not too bothered which side you might have been on in that skirmish of yours, just as long as it doesn't follow you here.'

'I doubt if anyone knows we are here and although we did steal the boat the only contact we have had was when Betsy acquired some food in Nantwich. By the way Betsy you never did tell me how you managed that.'

'Later Solomon, it's not a tale to be told in front of children.'

I looked at her quizzically but the folk in the hut laughed and most of them left us to rest although Arthur stayed to ask us questions about what we knew of the local troubles.

'It seems Nantwich is packed with Parliamentarian troops,' I said and then described what happened to us and the baggage train.

'Chester is still held by the Royalists,' said Arthur and we could probably get you there if you wish, although the weather seems to be brewing up and we may have to wait for the wind to die down as the estuary can be a very dangerous place in a storm.'

Arthur was right about the weather as we were unable to move from the island for ten days in which time we became acquainted with these gentle but hardy marsh people.

They made their living by fishing and in the summer months they would do reed cutting for thatching. During the three months either side of Christmas they were almost completely cut off although, if they really wanted to, they could make dry land.

They provisioned themselves during the summer and although this was a bleak and wild place it also had its own natural beauty. The marshes were full of bird life, fish and eels while the estuary provided shellfish and driftwood. So remote was this place that after a few days we felt relaxed and safe. We knew we would have to move as soon as the weather improved but our stay was enlightening in more ways than one.

Our relationship grew in those few days from acquaintances in adversity to lovers, which surprised Betsy as much as me. We were given the use of a small hut, which was warm and surprisingly dry considering the fact that water surrounded us on all sides and one night, while eating next to our fire, I asked Betsy to tell me about herself and I realised later that telling the tale brought us closer together.

'I am the bastard daughter of the Lord of our Manor. I never lived with him although he supported my mother financially. We lived in the village near the Manor and although he knew who I was he never tried to contact me. My mother was never angry about the arrangement and just accepted that this was her lot and she loved me dearly. My mother married when I was ten and her husband always treated me well. However the Roundheads threw the Lord off his Manor and confiscated his land and properties. We lived in one of his cottages and were forced out. There were fights and a small uprising against the Parliamentarians and both of my parents were killed. I was pretty enough and old enough to be thought a prize and the commander of the Parliamentarians took me into his household. I was fortunate that he did not harm me but I was forever seething with hate towards him for what he had done to my mother.

One night I crept into his room and slit his throat. I escaped and fell in with a passing troop of Royalists who took me to the tavern where you found me. I have been there for a year and have been using my time and talents to try and build up some cash to free myself from being a camp follower. This small horde I have strapped in a belt around my waist so if you ever have any amorous ideas make sure I don't think you are just after my money.'

We both laughed and fell into each other's arms in a passionate embrace. My first passionate embrace; never to be forgotten. When we got down to the money belt we again rolled around in laughter before making love on the floor of our own wooden hut.

Over the next few days we had great difficulty in keeping our hands off each other and each night was a new and wonderful experience. I think we both knew we were not in love but more just in need of affection in these otherwise dark times, while the villagers made fun of our obvious reactions towards each other. The day we had to move on was tinged with sadness at leaving our newly found friends and disrupting our newly cemented relationship. I had spent a memorable few days helping or hindering the catching of fish and collecting shellfish while Betsy had joined in with preparing food and playing with the children, but now the time had come to continue our journey.

Our aim was to get to Chester where I hoped I could find out what had happened to Luke while Betsy was keen to get to a town with the facilities for her trade.

The village boatmen took us out into the estuary and along to a port they knew was held by Royalists. From there they said we should be able to travel south safely to Chester. They provided us with some food and secretly dropped us off a mile from the port on a sandy beach. We said our farewells, thanked them again for their kindness and walked across the dunes towards the port.

We were soon confronted by Cavalry who escorted us to the road before crossing the river to the Bridgegate entrance of the city, which was flanked by two massive towers. We entered through a narrow passage that opened up to reveal the centre of the city. Black and white timber houses stood out in front of us with the Cathedral looming up behind. Around us there was much hectic activity with people rushing to and fro and horses and carts vying for room on the narrow streets. We were taken to a large building, which was being used as the command centre for the city and the cavalry officer who had taken us in introduced us to an officer at the door who took a message inside. After a few minutes wait we were delighted to see Captain Clarke ready to greet us.

The Captain explained that the skirmish had led to a retreat to Chester with a large loss of life as well as the loss of the baggage train.

'We have taken an inventory of the men lost and we believed you must be one of them. I am pleased you are both safe as I am sure is the man standing behind you,' I turned around to see Luke standing there with a huge grin on his face.

We embraced with a back slapping hug before Luke, looking at the lovely Betsy remarked, 'and I thought you were in trouble, while all the time you had the lovely Betsy as a companion; some people have all the luck.' We all laughed and Betsy gave Luke a kiss on the cheek.

Captain Clarke told us to find lodgings with Luke and then come back to report what had happened. This we did after telling Luke most of our story. He guessed the bit I missed out and he then told his tale of how the skirmish disintegrated into a rout and a rapid retreat. He had saved the two children and their mother had also somehow escaped with the help of the Cavalry but many men had lost their lives and the officers were all talking about the dramatic setback they had incurred.

In the days that followed we looked after the two horses which Luke had managed to save from the skirmish and from the information gleaned from others we decided we should move on to Lathom as soon as possible. Betsy had decided to stay behind and had already found a job serving in a tavern and after a little persuasion she allowed me to give her a few pounds to help her on her way. She was reluctant for obvious reasons but we both knew our relationship was one of real friends and everlasting.

After a sad parting Luke and I set off away from the City hoping that our journey north would not be as eventful as in the past although we were not that confident, due to the ever changing situation in Cheshire and Lancashire.

Chapter Four

THE SIEGE
(February to May 1644)

I felt very relieved to see the sight of Lathom house appearing in the distance through the trees. It had taken us over six months to complete a journey that in more normal times would have taken a few days. When we reached the edge of the wood we could see the road leading to the fortified house just a few hundred yards to our left. We stopped to analyse our next move. There was a lot of activity around the house and along the road. Carts pulled by oxen were streaming towards the house and around the base of the outer wall a large group of men were obviously improving the defences.

'Halt right there you two,' came a shout from behind.

We were soon surrounded by bowmen and musketeers who must have been watching us approach the house.

'I have a letter for The Earl of Derby from Oxford,' I said quickly hoping that this would ease the tension of the moment.

'That may be so young squire, but I would be grateful if you could both slowly dismount so that we may verify your claim.'

We dismounted and were disarmed before being led towards the house. Our captors made no attempt to converse with us but I felt we were being believed by the lack of aggression shown towards us.

Moving along the roads and marching past slow or queuing carts it was obvious that food and fodder was being brought to the house in some quantity.

Alongside the front gate, between the wall and the moat, men were hammering in spikes and assembling a palisade about six feet high. The moat was a wide one at around eight yards and the dirty water looked deep. On the face of it this fortified house was establishing considerable defences.

As we approached the gates four guards were ordered to stand with us while the rest of the troop returned to their lookout duty. We all stood back to allow two carts to pass across the narrow bridge, one coming out the other going in. I noticed three young children watching from the side of the bridge just as the two carts approached each other. It seemed one cart handler was having problems negotiating the manoeuvre and suddenly the two carts struck each other with the back end of one swinging around knocking one of the children straight into the moat. Our guards, Luke and I ran over to the scene just in time to see the boy go down under the water. I didn't hesitate but jumped in feet first after him. The water was deeper than I was tall but I am a good swimmer and quickly groped around unsuccessfully searching for the child. I surfaced, the child hadn't.

'To your left,' shouted Luke whereupon I dived under and suddenly felt clothing which I grabbed and hauled the child to the surface. I then swam to the side of the moat where strong arms pulled us both out. The boy lay still and everyone stood around in shock. I grabbed hold of his arms and stood up with him across my shoulders with his head down my back. I shook him up and down as violently as I could and to my relief the boy started spluttering and coughing. People were rushing across the bridge to help and they quickly helped restore the boy enough for him to sit up on his own.

'Edward are you alright?' spoke a soft but firm voice. 'What on earth happened?'

'Madam if I could explain,' said our guard leader. 'Young Edward here was knocked into the moat when two carts clashed on the road and this young man jumped in and saved his life.'

'Young man, although I do not know your name; I wish to thank you most sincerely on behalf of my husband, the Earl, and myself?'

'It is some time since we met Lady Charlotte and I would be surprised if you recognised me. I am Solomon Hawke and I am pleased young Edward is safe.'

'My dear Solomon of course it is you but how you have grown and such a fine looking young man. Again I must thank you for what you did but why are you here at such a dangerous time?'

'I have come with a letter to the Earl from my father my lady.'

'Let us go inside and we will read the letter as my husband is away at the moment.'

We entered the house passing through the gate, which emphasised the great depth of the stone walls. In the centre of a busy inner courtyard was a tall and imposing tower (I later found it to be called the Eagle Tower) and on either side were a number of lower buildings. We entered one, which turned out to be the main residence of the family, and by the time we arrived there was a crowd of people all wanting to know what had happened and asking if the boy was safe. Lady Charlotte quickly apprised them of the situation and Luke and I were ushered in by the guard leader and some servants.

Lady Charlotte spoke to the guard leader who left although before doing so he thanked me personally for my quick action. I introduced Luke and Lady Charlotte was quick to say that we were most welcome and that we would soon be shown to our rooms where I could change out of my dripping clothes. I passed the letter to Lady Charlotte who read it quickly.

'You are welcome to stay as long as you wish according to your father's wishes Solomon but firstly I must warn you of our situation here. Lancashire is rapidly showing more and more support for the Parliamentarian cause and we are informed that a force has been deployed against us and it could arrive very soon. Lord Derby is away in Ireland but I do not intend to simply present the house to anyone. As you can see Solomon, if you stay here you will be in the middle of an island surrounded by a sea of danger. We will talk more of this later but now I must check on Edward, in the mean time my housekeeper will assign you and Luke to appropriate accommodation.'

There was obviously not much room in the house for unexpected guests but the housekeeper led us to two rooms, which were probably servant's quarters. Two young men brought in our packs from the horses and others brought water for washing. A knock on the door a few minutes later revealed a tall bearded man who introduced himself as James the head of the household servants.

'Lady Charlotte has asked if both of you could dine with her in about two hours gentlemen and I have looked out a few extra clothes for you in case you were inconvenienced by your most heroic dip in our moat.' Obviously a man of some humour James handed us a pile of clothes and withdrew with a wry smile on his face.

After washing and changing Luke and I left our rooms and wandered out into the courtyard where many people were employed moving cattle and sheep around the pens on one side, stacking bales of hay against a far wall or emptying the carts which we had seen on the road. No one took much notice of us although two ladies thanked us for saving the young boy. The walls had no obvious cannons but we noticed hides covering some heaps along the parapet set back from the crenulated walls which could be cannons but which were hidden from any outside view. A number of men at arms were active in the courtyard but only a handful was manning the towers or walls. I was coming to the conclusion that this house with its towers, high wall, moat and other obstacles was now more of a castle than just the fortified house I had stayed in just three years before. Luke pointed out the blacksmith hard at work and when we walked over we could see he was making arrowheads and his assistants were moulding musket balls.

The dining hall was well furnished if a little bare but the food was excellent and a great treat after our time on the road. Lady Charlotte then introduced all her family, which included Edward five and William who was four, Amelia eleven and Henrietta who was the eldest at fourteen. Major Farmer was introduced to us as a Scottish Gentleman with military experience who had been placed in charge of the defence of the household and it was he who started the conversation by asking us about our journey. He seemed particularly interested in what troop movement we had seen and any gossip we had found out in the towns and villages. Lady Charlotte obviously wanted the conversation to move away from military manoeuvres and asked about my family. The girls remembered my brothers and I told them of their exploits and pointed out that neither was married and a wink towards the girls brought a chuckle from everyone. The children left us at the end of the meal and we moved to a comfortable sitting room next to the dining hall.

'Solomon I would like to explain our situation more fully to you after which you must decide if you wish to stay or leave. We have recently given over all of our estates to the Parliamentarians but I have persuaded them to allow me to stay in the house for the time being. I know this will not last and they will soon attempt to forcibly remove us all. I intend to resist for as long as possible with every resource at my disposal. We are bound to be heavily outnumbered and could be under siege for some time. Once under siege it may be difficult to get out and away from this area, where many of the landowners are now joining the Roundheads or pleading neutrality and are unlikely to be of any assistance to us. We are at present, gradually building up our provisions although much of this has to be done at night and I have asked our skilled Major to maintain and develop our military strength.'

Farmer joined in the explanation by stating that men had been secretly entering the house over the last few days and he hoped for a garrison of around three hundred loyal men at arms would be reached very soon.

'Now you see our plight you must take your time and decide whether you feel you should stay or go,' Lady Charlotte concluded.

I glanced at Luke who seemed to understand what I was going to say (a habit I increasingly found unnerving during our time together) and he nodded almost imperceptibly.

'Lady Charlotte, I was sent to you to be away from a particularly unpleasant situation by my father who hoped you would be kind enough to take me into your household until the situation changes. You have welcomed us into your home and it would be an honour if we could serve you in any way you feel fit,' I replied.

Over the next few days more work was done to fortify the house but most of the traffic into the house now came at night. Luke and I were given no specific jobs to start with but we helped with the horses, which numbered thirty and joined in the weapons and fighting practices with the men at arms. These generally seemed to be experienced men with a high level of skill in shooting and general fighting although those that had swords were given extra practice by one of Farmer's six lieutenants. I felt this was where I could be the most use and Lieutenant Page was quick to see the potential in me and I progressed to doing much of the tutoring. Despite the regular bangs and bruises and a couple of broken fingers, the sword troop enjoyed the training, which became highly competitive. One of the troop stood out as an excellent swordsman and also a strong and skilful fighter named Duncan MacDonald, one of a handful of Scots in our force. During practice most of the others would try to avoid Duncan who usually dealt out a quick lesson often resulting in his opposition finishing up on their backside.

He was a fighter, a man of experience and I used him as a role model for others to imitate. In the end I was the only one willing and really able enough to give Duncan any sort of meaningful practice and when I did get the upper hand I doubted if Duncan was fighting at his optimum.

'How can you beat a fighter like Duncan?' one of the troops called out one day after he had been pinned against the wall by the Scotsman.

'Solomon, Sir what would you do?' called another. This is how the troop addressed me, as my position in the household was rather difficult to place.

I had been set up by the troop who wanted Duncan and me to compete seriously. We generally used heavy wooden swords for practice and with these readily at hand we agreed that a body blow would win. I was excited but rather apprehensive, as I never thought Duncan was really exerting himself in our previous fights. Surrounded by the troop we circled slowly looking for the right moment. Duncan came at me fast, very fast and I only just managed to parry his swinging blows. He followed up with a series of lunges, which I dodged while moving back and sideways quickly. This was my only asset; speed.

Duncan was stronger and more experienced but I decided to continue to defend and wait for a chance to counter attack. I dodged; he lunged and swung strongly. I parried and moved fast. I felt Duncan was tiring and after one of his thrusts I attacked with three quick swings to his body he parried two and before my third was half way complete he stung my chest with a stab and then fended off my blow. I had lost. The troop cheered and congratulated us both on a good fight. Duncan and I both breathing heavily moved to a bench nearby and sat down to recover and take a greatly appreciated drink.

'You were doing the right thing,' said Duncan who had obviously worked out my plan.

'Next time, do not be so impatient, another few minutes and I may well have lost to your tactics.'

I rather doubted his conclusion but I hoped I never had to put his theory to the test in real life.

Most of our time was taken up with the military activity and Luke seemed to be enjoying his assignment as sharpshooter in one of the towers. On one occasion I noticed him pacing out the ground in front of the house with a bucket of lime in his hand. Every now and then he would paint one side of a stone with the white side facing the tower. I went over to the parapet on his return to hear him explaining to the archers and musketeers how to use these distance markers to help with accuracy.

There was for me one major and very pleasant diversion from my duties and that involved a particular member of a family who were smuggled into the house two weeks after our own arrival. The family name was Kent and this comprised of father and two daughters. They turned out to be local landowners who had been forced out of their home by the Parliamentarians. It seems they were lucky to escape and had arrived seeking shelter. Lady Charlotte seemed only too happy to take them in and I was certainly happy with the arrangement as I developed a somewhat romantic if platonic relationship with their eldest daughter Rebecca. I say romantic, but at the time it was more a case of me trying to meet her whenever I could and her being just friendly and kind to me. My heart seemed to beat double time every time I was near her and I felt I was blushing when anyone brought her into a conversation. She soon noticed and after a period of teasing me began to take my affections more seriously and we both tried to be together whenever possible. Together was fine but alone together was a rare event as younger sister Lucy acted as a virtually permanent chaperone.

Rebecca was tall with hair the colour of sun ripened wheat and quite the most beautiful young woman I had ever met. She was unusually active and strong for a woman mainly due to her love of riding and the work she had done with her father on their estate. Her outwardly friendly nature made her an instant hit with everyone and my troop certainly enjoyed employing some gentle teasing at my expense.

We were now all confined to the house as information had been received that a large force was moving through southern Lancashire and could be heading in our direction.

Later on we found out that the leaders of the force had not told their men where they were going in case some decided that they did not want to attack a house run by a Lady with whom many had had friendly dealings in the past. It is said the men found out their destination when a preacher recited a chapter from Jeremiah and made reference to Lady Charlotte and Lathom, which he likened to Babylon. Lady Charlotte was thereafter quite often referred to as Babylon although not within her earshot. The men within the walls seemed proud of the fact that their lady was seemingly a revered opponent to the Parliamentarians.

Our fortifications were now in place although we had less gunpowder than hoped for. The cannon on the parapets and towers along with the potential musket fire would create a powerful enfilade. The one unusual feature of the whole defence was that little was obvious to an outside observer. Farmer made sure that at any one time only a few men were visible on the walls and the cannon were well hidden.

At the end of February the enemy made camp two miles from Lathom and the next day a Parliamentarian captain came to deliver a message from Sir Thomas Fairfax their commander in chief. The vast majority of our men were hidden in the towers and house buildings when he arrived with his escort.

Lady Charlotte greeted them and I stood with her household while she read the terms offered out loud.

'Fairfax wishes me to leave the house and go with his men for a meeting. My answer is that I will consider his proposals but wonder, considering his relative low birth, should it not be me summoning him to meet with me. I expect a week to think about the proposal. Now Captain I suggest you return quickly with my answer or I might consider the head of a messenger on a pike would send the same message.'

Seeing the determined demeanour of Lady Charlotte the Captain turned trying to retain his dignity and walked rapidly out of the fortress.

A few days later Lady Charlotte agreed to allow two Colonels into the fortress with a promise to return them safely. Lady Charlotte then ordered all her Lieutenants to meet her and the Major in the house. I was invited to attend her briefing.

'Gentlemen we are to be visited today by Fairfax's Colonels and I would like to give them a surprise. When they arrive I want you to put on a show of strength, which may then make them think again before attacking us immediately. Attack us they will soon enough but we have a few other surprises in store for them and I would like to delay them for as long as possible.'

At noon the Colonels and their small escort arrived at the gates which were opened with a flourish to reveal not just a lady and her household servants but a phalanx of men at arms in the courtyard and a line of officers and men leading from the gateway entrance to the great hall where on the steps stood the resplendent Major in his finest attire. Casting their gaze around, the Colonels could see the towers and parapets bristling with arms, cannon and well disciplined men. They were ushered into the great hall to the imposing sight of the Countess surrounded by her women and with her children at her side

The Colonels were regally invited to sit and read out their terms. Lady Charlotte refused to accept any of them and the Colonels were in no position to insist. They left confused and wondering how they could be so badly informed as to the real nature of the fortress and its defences.

In the days following the visit the Parliamentarians began siege preparations by digging trenches and banks for troops and cannon.

I watched with Luke from one of the towers as cannon were brought closer and musketeers took up their positions.

When the first cannon shot occurred it took us all by surprise and we wondered what effect they would have on the walls. During the first day about thirty blasts from the cannons had been aimed at the wall close to the tower but it was difficult to see what effect they were having. Some muskets were fired but we did not respond.

Lieutenant Page greeted us on the palisade and enquired:

'What about the range Luke? Could your sharpshooters do some damage around the cannon?'

'Yes Sir I am sure we could make a few hits.'

'Good. There is a plan for my troop to go out and spike the cannons but we need to scare off their musketeers to give our men time to do the job.'

'Solomon I need you and five picked men to take spiking equipment out to the guns. The rest of our troop will go with you to provide cover. We will have to work quickly so go to the blacksmith who will explain what to do, select your men and be ready to move in two hours.'

I raced across to where Duncan was sitting on some steps and explained the plan.

'I will get the other four men Solomon and we will meet at the blacksmiths.'

The burly blacksmith showed how to do the task and provided mallets and spikes. We all wore swords, which we decided to take with us although they could hinder our speed of progress.

On Lieutenant Page's order the sharpshooters blasted off two rapid volleys at the soldiers around the cannons. Luke had suggested that each man have two firearms with another man at arms aiding the reloading to increase the speed of shooting. This rapid and accurate firing must have had the desired effect because when the gates were thrown open and our covering troop ran out we could see men streaming away from the cannons. We all ran the two hundred yards as quickly as possible and the musketeers charged the now thin line of defenders. My spiking group reached the cannons only to find them abandoned. We quickly hammered metal spikes into the powder hole of the six cannon closest to us. A fight was taking place to our left as musketeers from both sides had taken their shot and were now dealing in hand to hand combat. On completing our task I shouted to the Lieutenant who ordered a retreat. This became easier after Duncan and the rest of us decided to charge the defenders from the side and cause a distraction. Not knowing how many of us there were the defenders turned on their heels and ran. We all jogged back to the gate under covering fire from the towers. One of our men had been killed and was being carried by his compatriots but it was quite obvious the Parliamentarians had suffered far greater losses including the use of six cannons for the near future.

Over the next few days the few remaining cannons shelled our walls until one morning an explosion, far louder than a normal cannon, went off and a huge ball sailed clean over the walls and landed in the courtyard on the far side of the house. There was some panic amongst the people in the courtyard and I saw Major Farmer running towards the parapet to see what had fired the missile so much further than the normal cannon.

'That's a mortar,' said Duncan who was standing with Luke and me in one of the towers. 'They could send cannon balls and rocks right into the residence and possibly even fireballs.'

The mortar only fired six times during that first day but we had little protection against its bombs, although men were issued with hides to cover any fires that might break out. Lady Charlotte moved herself, many of the women and all the children of the fortress into Eagle Tower where they would be relatively safe.

'Something must be done about the mortar,' said Lady Charlotte to Farmer and his lieutenants who had been assembled in

Eagle Tower's main hall.' Does anyone have a suggestion?'

'Could we steal it,' I heard myself say. Luke and I had been discussing the mortar and we felt that removing it altogether would have a demoralising effect on the Parliamentarians and also boost the flagging spirit of some of our defenders.

'It weighs half a ton Solomon,' said the Major, 'but it could be done. I think that with enough manpower we could pull it up the road as long as we are covered for about an hour.'

No other ideas were muted and Lady Charlotte was positively excited by the idea of dealing her opponents such a stinging blow.

'If the Major believes it is feasible without risking too much I suggest we carry this out as soon as possible.'

It was decided to make a full-scale attack on the Parliamentarians. We had twenty cavalrymen and nearly three hundred men at arms and two hundred were made ready for the attack. Covering fire would be given by our cannon, which had been used sparingly due to our shortage of powder, and by sharpshooters on the towers and walls. Lieutenant Page was placed in charge of bringing in the mortar and this was to be hauled up the road by every available man and a few women, which probably added up to around eighty people in total. The Lieutenant put our troop in charge of the haulage and protection of the rope pullers.

The sight of nearly every man and woman in the fortress all gathering in their groups inside the courtyard readying themselves for the action is one that I shall always clearly remember. There was at first an air of excitement probably brought about by fear but the chatter showed a confidence in the proposed action. We had been confined to the fortress for weeks and were now all going to charge out against an army of Parliamentarians who had over ten times our number.

Charlotte stood on the residence steps and addressed us all in her usual commanding but caring way. This brought a cheer from the throng followed by an immediate crash of the cannons. The main gates were flung open and through the smoke charged our small cavalry troop. Men at arms streamed out after them and the musket and cannon fire from above us was deafening.

'Let's go,' ordered Lieutenant Page and our rope pullers all trotted down the road after us. We didn't have much time to see how the skirmish was going but we were not fired upon and we soon arrived at the abandoned mortar. This was a stubby barrelled, but very heavy cannon on a truck of four wheels. Men quickly tied the ropes around the wooden frame and the well-organised gang started moving it over its defensive wall and onto the road. This was done without too many problems and then the long pull up the road began. Meanwhile Duncan and I with the rest of the troop lined the battle side of the road looking out for possible aggressors. From here we could see the attack was going well. All the parliamentarians who must have been caught by complete surprise were running away towards their camp followed by our musketeers who were firing amongst their midst and our riders who were hacking their way through knots of defenders. It took us nearly an hour to bring the mortar through the fortress gates by which time the retreat of our men was well under way.

The cavalry were the last to enter the gates as the sharpshooters continued to give covering fire from the towers. Our injured were carried in by the men at arms and were helped into the residence where some of the women had created an infirmary in expectation.

We lost three men and had twenty slightly wounded whereas Farmer estimated the Parliamentary losses could be as many as two hundred. This was a major victory and for the next week we were not harassed in any way. The mortar was placed in the middle of the courtyard and although it was of little military use to us the fact that many passers-by aimed a kick at it often followed by a laugh showed that it had a different kind of value.

Eventually the Parliamentarians resumed bombarding the walls with chain and shot but they did not seem to be having much effect. I took my duties seriously but I was also getting very serious about Rebecca. I found her easy to talk to but not so easy to resist. I wanted to hold her every time I saw her but usually had to be satisfied with holding hands and a rare kiss. One day while sitting around an open fire at the back of the courtyard Rebecca said did I know the reason the tall tower had its name. I said I thought it was because it was so high in the sky and was such a good look out place.

'One of the ancestors had an affair with a local gentlewoman who had a baby boy. The baby was taken away by a trustworthy servant and laid under a tall tree on the estate where eagles were often seen. The lady of the house, who was unable to have children, found the baby by accident, or design, while out walking and describing it as a miracle, adopted the child who became the heir to the estate. The Earl is the descendent of this boy.'

'I am not sure if that is a happy or sad tale but I always thought babies were found under bushes anyway.'

Rebecca gave me a more than playful smack on the shoulder and we both burst into laughter at my rather clumsy way of bringing up the subject of intimacy.

The siege came to an abrupt halt when one morning I awoke to shouts from men on the walls. I quickly dressed and ran from my quarters to investigate the reason for the noise. My worst thoughts expected it to be an attack but in fact it seemed that the Parliamentarians had completely withdrawn and disappeared from view. Major Farmer sent a troop of cavalry to investigate and on their return it was made clear that they had indeed removed themselves from the vicinity. Two troops of horsemen were sent out to gather more information and they in turn returned in mid-afternoon but this time they were accompanied by a large Royalist force of cavalry and infantry.

From my vantage point on the tower I could clearly see the regal and resplendent figure of Prince Rupert at the head of the column of cavalry, which on arrival deployed itself at various points around the house while the infantry made camp close to the Parliamentarians' recent position.

The men at arms of the house and the civilian population which together added up to over four hundred people cheered excitedly as the Prince and his entourage appeared through the gateway. The Prince was welcomed into the house with his lieutenants who were then all escorted into the residence for an audience with Lady Charlotte.

I had joined in the cheering with Luke at my side but my initial feelings of relief and euphoria were dashed as I spotted one particular cavalry officer dismount in the courtyard. Nicolas Caxton, who was the reason for me being at Lathom, was now here in what I had come to feel was my second home. Luke also spotted him and pulled me back into a doorway out of sight.

'Looks as though your friend has followed us,' said Luke.

'Well let's keep out of his way for now. Come on we'll go and find out the news from some of the men outside.'

The courtyard was now full of noisy and excited people, which included Rebecca and her family. Rather unexpectedly she ran over and hugged me before planting a kiss on my cheek and saying, 'at last we are free of these dreadful Roundheads, perhaps we will soon be able to go home.'

I could see the look of happiness in her face but she must have noticed my lack of excitement and enquired:

'What is the matter Solomon you don't seem very pleased?'

'I am totally delighted the Prince has come to our rescue but it was the siege that brought us together and your freedom is now likely to split us up.'

'It doesn't have to be like that surely Solomon, perhaps you could come with us and I know my father would be only too pleased to welcome you into our household.'

'It may not be as simple as that Rebecca, but let's not worry about that now. We are off to find out the news from the cavalry outside. Do you want to join us?'

'I think I will stay with Lucy for now but come back and tell me any news you can find out about our home.'

I said I would and Luke and I went out of the house to where we soon came across a few men resting their horses in the field close by. Their news was mixed. On their journey to relieve us they had come across a number of Roundhead troops but none had fully engaged them. It seemed they were checking on their strength and it is rumoured the Parliamentarians might try to engage the main army in the near future. We could find out nothing specific about Rebecca's home but it seemed unlikely that she would be able to go home in the near future.

We decided to return to the house and on making the bend into the gate ran straight into Caxton and the other two Lieutenants I had met at the archery competition who were leading their horses out of the courtyard.

Both sides stopped in our tracks and I surprised myself by speaking first.

'Good afternoon Gentlemen, and good afternoon Caxton,' I said with more bravado than I actually felt.

Luke chuckled at my side but Caxton's face went red with rage and I am sure he would have attacked me if Major Farmer had not appeared from behind saying that he would like to talk with us in the residence.

We avoided any more eye contact with the Lieutenants and followed the Major into the residence where we were escorted into Lady Charlotte's hall.

'Solomon my dear I wish to tell you of a decision we have made and then you will have to decide on your next action. My household and that of Mr Kent will be leaving the house in the hands of the military as Prince Rupert has informed us that another and greater Parliamentary threat may be forthcoming. We will be travelling to the Earl's estate in the Isle of Man as soon as possible. I know your father wished you to come here but it is now for you to decide if you want to accompany us. On my family's part we would be grateful if you would join us and be part of our protection.'

I looked at Luke and as in the past I did not need a verbal answer from him and I repeated my loyalty to the lady and her family.

That evening I took my turn to check on the horses in the stables at the far end of the courtyard. It was dark except for the one lamp the stable boys had left hanging outside the main door. I unclipped the lamp, went in closed the door behind me and was duly hit hard across my shoulders. The lamp went out as it crashed to the floor and what seemed like numerous feet started kicking my body. I tried to get up but was pushed down and hit again. The last kick must have knocked me unconscious because the next thing I remember was Luke helping me to sit up.

'What happened to you Solomon?'

'I think there were three of them; they ambushed me as soon as I came in. I must have passed out,' I groaned, not quite knowing which part of my body to hold. I sat up painfully feeling a large bump on my head and I gasped at the pain in my side. I was in considerable discomfort as we decided I probably had no broken bones although my ribs were a cause for concern. We decided to visit Martha who had been tending the injured soldiers and on taking off my shirt she asked how I had been injured.

'I came off second in a fight Martha.'

After looking at my hands she made the observation, 'looks like a bit of a one sided affair to me.'

Martha asked Luke to fetch some snow from the ice house and on his return she wrapped it in a cloth and held it to my side while I held another package on my head. Martha then bandaged my ribs commenting on the fact that my well-muscled chest had saved me from having any breakages.

Luke and I returned to our lodgings to prepare for our journey where we bumped into James who quickly noticed my discomfort.

'What have you lads been up to then; been celebrating too hard?'

'Hardly celebrating,' said Luke who explained what had happened.

'Really, any idea who they were?' he asked.

'I could not be sure, it was dark and their faces were covered.'

'Can you remember any details; did they speak?' enquired James.

'No, but I do remember something about one of the boots as I ducked to try and avoid a kick in the head. In fact it seemed as if I were on the outside looking in as I remember thinking that I had never seen black spurs before.'

'Well that's not a lot to go on,' observed James. 'I suggest you get some rest before tomorrow's journey.'

This I did for around two hours while Luke cleaned the firearms and packed our saddlebags before a knock on the door revealed James who informed us that Lady Charlotte had asked for some extra protection and he had agreed to assign a Lieutenant and twenty men to accompany us to the Isle of Man. She had then surprisingly asked specifically for Nicholas Caxton a request agreed upon by the Prince. Lady Charlotte had explained that this young man had made 'a significant impression,' upon her Ladyship.

'Which in some ways he had,' added James. 'You see, Lady Charlotte found out about your adventure in the stables and asked me to look into it, after a short enquiry I found the owner of the black spurs and he is now rather reluctantly readying himself for a trip across the Irish Sea. Her Ladyship wanted to keep a close eye on the perpetrator of the violent attack. I believe she felt she would be more in control of the situation in her home on the Isle and I think the Lieutenant might be in for a rather large shock.'

I rather doubted the wisdom of Lady Charlotte's decision and I felt uneasy about the fact that the man I was told to avoid was now part of the same company as myself.

James seemed to sense my unease and pointed out, 'Lady Charlotte is a very astute woman, as I am sure you are now aware, she does not make decisions without much consideration. She was personally affronted by the fact that one of her guests had been assaulted and I think Caxton should feel rather more uncomfortable about the situation than yourself. I would suggest you let her sort out the problem before you decide to retaliate.'

Now that I knew Caxton was responsible for my beating I was determined that he would not get away with it but out of respect for Lady Charlotte I decided not to precipitate any action for now unless Caxton confronted me first.

Chapter Five

THE ISLE OF MAN
(June 1644)

We travelled to Liverpool under the protection of a section of Prince Rupert's force and embarked for the Isle of Man on two ships.

The main bulk of Lady Charlotte's household, Caxton and a number of men at arms boarded the larger of the two vessels sent by the Earl to transport his family to the Isle. This was a merchant carrier, which I was told had an impressive sixteen guns but was manned by a surprisingly small crew of forty seamen. Lady Charlotte was the last to be ferried across the roads along with her ladies in waiting, while Luke and I were assigned to the second vessel, which turned out to be a relatively roomy Dutch Fleut. I was pleased to see Rebecca and her family joining us along with Duncan and his troop of soldiers under the command of Lieutenant Page.

We were informed that the journey should take around 20 hours which would mean an overnight journey if we were to catch the next tide. The weather was also causing some concern, as although it was only mid afternoon when we weighed anchor it was already very dull with banks of clouds sweeping in from the West. The carrier shook out its sails and under the strong breeze moved swiftly across our bows and out into the main channel. After another half an hour a sudden burst of activity and a few rapid orders was followed by top—men running up the ratlines to release our sails. I was amazed at the sure-footed swiftness of the men who seemed to be precariously balanced on the spars high above us and the relatively few shouts of instructions required from the commanders of the ship. They were obviously a well-organised and professional crew and I felt somewhat relieved, as this was my first long sea voyage.

The Harrier, as our vessel was named, soon started to ride the swell and dive into the troughs in a startling manner. The feeling of power in the ship and the spray crashing over the bow was an experience I felt exhilarating which was certainly not how Luke would have described it. This was his first ever sea voyage and the heaving of the ship was now being followed by the heaving of his stomach and for the next few hours he spent most of the time spewing into the guttering under the ships gunwales. I stayed close, but not too close, just in case he got worse although as night drew in he seemed to gradually recover. This was one of the few times I have seen Luke unable to make some remark or another and I secretly hoped to use his inconvenience to my advantage at some time in the future.

We were given a small two bunk berth and I made Luke drink some water before encouraging him to go to sleep on the lower bunk as I felt sleeping underneath him could be fraught with dangers. I left him to sleep and visited Rebecca and her family who all seemed to be fine despite the rough ride. Over the next few hours the weather worsened considerably and I gingerly climbed up the ladder to the deck. It was now pitch black but while hanging on to the rail under the quarterdeck I could still clearly see huge waves crashing over the bow and water sweeping across the deck.

Unbelievably three men suddenly dropped down in front of me having been up in the shrouds taking in some of the sails. The deck lifted in front of me as we rode a massive wave and then for a moment we seemed to hang in the air before plunging down into a trough the height of the masts. I slipped as water cascaded over the deck and in losing my grip on the rail I started sliding towards the side of the ship until a strong hand on my collar hauled me to my feet.

'Haven't found your sea legs yet then?' said Duncan who was standing over me while hanging on to a shroud. 'Best we go below, it looks as if things are getting worse by the minute.'

We drunkenly climbed down the ladder and shut the door behind us just as the ship made a huge lurch. We both went crashing into the mess furniture and our world seemed almost upside down. With another almighty crash the ship must have righted itself as we were flung back towards the door where we fell together in a heap.

'Christ, are you all right?' asked Duncan.

'I think so,' I replied, although my ribs were suggesting otherwise. 'Let's find out if the others are safe.'

We found Luke on the floor holding his head but he assured us he was fine so we clambered through to Rebecca's berth, which was easier said than done with the ship lurching from side to side in what seemed like a corkscrew motion.

There was obviously much distress in Rebecca's family's cabin and her father seemed relieved to see us after we had lurched through the door.

'It's Rebecca,' he said shakily, 'she hit her head and is still unconscious. He was holding her in his arms and I could see blood oozing out of her ear, which had stained his shirt. The tears on his cheek emphasised how concerned he was as were the rest of the family who were huddled in the corner frightened and tearful.

'You stay here, I will inform the Captain and see what the situation is,' said Duncan who struggling against the violent movement of the ship clambered out of the cabin just as Luke made an appearance. Luke went immediately to the group in the corner while I tried to help Rebecca's father hold his daughter steady in the chaotic movement of the room.

Water was now cascading down the ladder-way and into the room, which was dark, except for a violently swinging lantern in the far corner. I could see no change in Rebecca and I took off my jacket to help keep her warm. We all stayed as we were for what seemed like hours until eventually Duncan returned.

'The Captain will send a man down as soon as he can but at the moment he has his hands full just keeping us afloat,' he whispered so as not to alarm the others. 'The storm is worsening and two men have already been badly injured. I am going back up to help where I can; will you be able to cope here?'

'It's Rebecca I am worried about, her breathing seems shorter and I am finding it difficult to keep her warm.'

Rebecca never regained consciousness although her breathing seemed to ease and we were all worried for her life. Her father and Lucy were distraught and I had not felt despair like this in my life. She was such a vibrant and loving girl who I had fallen in love with at first sight. Everyone loved and admired her and I for one felt hollow and inadequate.

The storm gradually died down and two seamen moved Rebecca to the small cabin next door where we made her as comfortable as possible. Luke stayed with Lucy and her father but nothing we could say could relieve the anguish we all felt.

It took another ten hours before we sighted the fort on St Michael's Isle, which the Earl had constructed to protect the harbour at Castletown and eventually we dropped anchor and were taken ashore by a flotilla of small boats.

Lady Charlotte met us at the landing stage and she embraced Lucy and her father before leading us to the nearby residence where Mr Kent explained what had happened. Her Ladyship looked across to me and I could see tears rolling down her cheek before she looked away to spend time with Lucy.

Rebecca was carried to the house where Her Ladyship promised the best of care.

I went to my room where James came to see me with food and drink. He was quieter than I had ever known him and he left after simply laying his hand on my shoulder.

In the morning I met up with Luke and Duncan who were talking to Lieutenant Page and a soldier I did not know but was introduced as Captain Farrow who expressed his hope for Rebecca's recovery and then made us a proposition.

'I am in charge of the defences for the Island which although relatively small has a long coastline, we have put in plans but I have been short of manpower and need an appraisal from another set of eyes as to any weaknesses there might be. I have put Lieutenant Page in charge and her Ladyship suggested that you might accompany him.'

'We leave in the morning with the troop,' said Lieutenant Page, please inform me of your decision this evening Solomon so that preparations can be made.

It was quite obvious that Lady Charlotte had made the arrangement to get me away from the residence and the solemn atmosphere but I was reluctant to leave while Rebecca was so ill.

'What do you think?' I asked Luke.

'I will do whatever you wish Solomon but I think we should go and be of some practical use and as we do not know how long we will be able to stay here safely, I would like to look around the countryside just in case we have to leave in a hurry?'

After some thought I agreed and said I would inform Mr Kent of my decision and Luke went off to tell the Lieutenant and start our preparations.

Mr Kent was fully in accordance with my decision and added;

'If you ever need my help Solomon and I am in a position to be of some assistance please do not hesitate to ask. I know how much you mean to Rebecca and I want you to think of us as part of your family.'

We embraced and I left to be on my own while I could. I walked out to the headland overlooking the harbour and sat amongst the buttercups in the grass on the hill. I felt so helpless and I just longed to see Rebecca again realising how much I missed her smiles and teasing. I lay on the hill for over an hour before walking back into town to prepare for our assignment.

Our troop left early in the morning and although I had not seen him, Luke said he had spotted Caxton in an Inn in the evening getting rather drunk and being his usual boorish self, another good reason to get out of the town.

During the first day we rode up the east coast of the Isle where the main threat seemed to come from and the coastline was a mixture of low lying land and sandy beaches or higher ground with low cliffs. The defences included towers, which held a hand-full of troops who welcomed us before pointing out their duties and the possible landing places. They also explained the rapid information system they used between towers, which included beacons and also fast horses.

We stopped overnight in the village alongside Douglas Bay, which was well defended by a number of small forts and cannon.

It took us eight days to complete our task and the Lieutenant took notes after discussions with the local troops and men in his own troop of whom Duncan was obviously the most knowledgeable. It was an enjoyable time riding with the men through the pleasant countryside and along the coastal routes and although I realised I was less than good company, I gradually began to feel able to talk about Rebecca to Luke who was turning into a good listener.

We arrived in Castletown and on reaching the Earl's residence we were met by Captain Farrow who took the Lieutenant away for a debriefing. After dealing with the horses we took our baggage to our rooms but before we could decide what to do next we were met by James who said the Earl wished to see us as soon as possible.

We accompanied James who informed us that Mr Kent had decided to take Rebecca to friends in France where she could be cared for away from the present unstable situation. This rather took me aback and I stopped in my tracks for a moment to take in the information. This seemed to draw a line under the recent past, which I was reluctant to let go although perhaps I could travel to France with the Kent family.

My confused thoughts were interrupted by The Earl greeting us and thanking us for being part of the reconnaissance party and then he invited us to take a seat.

'I have information from the mainland which concerns your family Luke. Your father and his household have left the country and taken refuge with friends in France. It seems that even around Oxford the dangers are growing. The other news is about your brother Thomas. As far as we know he has been captured by the Parliamentarians and taken to the prison in Lancaster Castle.'

'How did this happen?'

'His troop was attacked and captured while scouting for Prince Rupert. I do not know what will befall him but I would imagine they will try him for treason at some time in the near future.'

'What can we do, we must do something to help?'

'Well I am not sure we can do much but I do have the men who brought the message and they followed the captors to the prison which they said is not well defended as there was only a handful of prisoners. I asked them if they thought we could send a rescue party and they agreed it might be possible. They would also wish to be included in any attempt you make, as both of them owed your brother a favour. We obviously cannot send a large force and in fact I believe this is a task for a small group which might be able to get close to the prison with less likelihood of being noticed.'

'Count me in,' said Luke without hesitation, 'but I would feel more confident if we had a trained soldier to lead us.'

We looked at each other and I knew whom Luke was thinking about.

'If you can find someone who would go you can take him with my blessing although I would rather you leave me with my officers who are too few as it is. The two men are with Captain Farrow and I can assure you they are very able and can be trusted totally.'

'I will go and speak with Duncan,' suggested Luke.

'Good idea I will meet you later after I have found our two volunteers.'

I had found myself making the decision automatically despite my earlier thoughts of travelling to France to be with Rebecca.

On meeting Sam North and Joe Spencer I knew immediately that these were indeed men we could trust. They greeted me with respect in their voice and wide smiles on their faces.

'We are keen to help you rescue your brother Sir, as without his help neither of us would be here today.'

'I am grateful to you both but how do you know Thomas?'

'We fought with Prince Rupert as pike men at Edgehill but were unlucky enough to get involved with another officer who accused us of theft. It was only an intervention by your brother that saved us. He went out of his way to find the real culprit and stood up to the other officer's bullying. If found guilty we would surely have been hung that day.'

'What was the officer's name?' I asked.

'Caxton,' replied Sam, 'Lieutenant Nicholas Caxton.'

Chapter Six

THE RESCUE
(Jun/July 1644)

Rebecca and her family sailed for France two days later having left details of their destination followed by many embraces and tears.

The five of us had a relatively uneventful journey back to the mainland although Luke, still suffering from seasickness, complained he thought he was near to death for the first few hours.

We sailed into Morecambe Bay and eventually the mouth of the River Kent and although we had seen some other vessels there were none that caused any consternation for the Captain who eventually anchored his vessel in the middle of the river and then launched a boat to take us ashore. We knew that to the south the Parliamentarians had now gained a strong hold on Lancashire, but

Carlisle to the north and Cumbria in general were still in favour of the King and the Earl had written some letters of introduction to some of his colleagues in the area. We were first to travel to Levens Hall, which Sam and Joe knew about and which was only a few miles from our landing place.

We decided to try to hire a cart to take us and our baggage the fifteen miles to the hall and Joe and Sam went off to find one. We found an inn where we would all meet up and Luke and I went in for some refreshment while Duncan stated he would be back soon and without explanation walked off down the road after leaving his baggage with us.

I had been reflecting on our circumstances for some time but the right time to discuss it with Luke had not arrived until now. I felt I needed to gain Luke's assurance that he felt he was doing the right thing

'Our situation has changed somewhat Luke since my father gave us instructions to travel to Lathom. We are now on our own and although I know I must try to help Tom I am not sure where we are likely to go after that. I feel I must commit myself to the King's cause but I do not want to drag you into something you feel uncomfortable with.'

'I appreciate your concern Sol but let's do one thing at a time. We must find a way of releasing Tom and then if we are still free to make a choice I am sure it will be clearer by then. As to the 'I' and 'we,' let's make sure we stick together as I think we have a greater chance of surviving this mess if we watch out for each other. I am sure Duncan will have a few ideas and maybe he will be able to help us decide our future moves.'

I bought Sam and Joe a drink when they returned with a cart and as we chatted I found out more about our two new companions.

'I am the son of a blacksmith from Leicestershire and have been working for Prince Rupert along with Sam here as a sort of special agent,' said Joe.

Sam continued by saying; 'The Prince gives us tasks that he feels ordinary soldiers would not be able to handle and I must say this one certainly sounds pretty difficult.'

'What did you do before you joined The Prince then Sam?' I asked.

'I was a Master's Mate on a trading vessel out of Liverpool and The Prince recruited me after I had helped him during a bit of a skirmish off the coast of Wales.'

'Saved the Prince's life he did,' retorted Joe, 'and got injured in the process.'

'Well I am fine now thanks to the fact that I was one of only a few who could actually swim that day; you would think a Prince could swim wouldn't you?'

'Don't know as that follows Sam I once knew a shepherd who hated sheep,' responded Joe without a flicker of a smile on his face.

We all sat in silence for a few moments trying to figure out the connection when Duncan reappeared and sat down with a drink.

'Your Brother is in the Gate House prison of Lancaster Castle which is basically a debtors' jail. We need to get there as soon as possible as rumours have it that prisoners are either tried and hung for treason or moved back to Manchester where the prisons are more secure.'

Shortly afterwards we gathered up our baggage, bought some food from the inn and made our way slowly to Levens Hall. It was a hot, dry journey and although we only stopped a few times to water, feed and rest the two nags, which slowly pulled us along; it took us until the early evening to reach our destination.

Sam had described the place to us along the way and Joe had recounted a ghost story related to the hall after which Duncan rather snorted that as long as we did not run into a Gypsy with a black dog we should be safe. Our chuckles at his gruff Scottish nature were met with a baleful stare although we all found it hard not to burst out laughing our attention was soon draw to the parkland and house on the horizon.

'The owner is Alan Bellingham and I have letters of introduction from The Earl. The Prince has often called on him before for assistance and he is a loyal supporter of the King. We are to ask for horses and perhaps a stay for a night before we move on in the morning,' I informed everyone.

'Well, here comes the reception committee,' said Luke pointing to a group of riders emanating from the grounds near the house.

The riders greeted us and after reading my note of introduction escorted us to the house whereupon we were met by three immaculately dressed royalist soldiers standing on the steps of the house. They informed us that the owner was away but having read the missive from The Earl said they would provide horses and tack and that we could bed down in the stable area along with the other troops.

In the late evening we all ate together
with the soldiers and managed to gain more
information about the local and national
situation. It seemed that a number of conflicts
had not gone well and the Parliamentarians
had gained control of most of the Midlands
and the North whilst the King had his strength
in the west of the country including my home
area of Oxford. It was becoming obvious that
travelling to Lancaster would be difficult
and we needed a plan, which would allow us
to penetrate Parliamentarian held areas. We
had about 20 miles to travel through enemy
territory before trying to find a way to release
Tom from a probably well-policed jail and
we definitely needed a plan.

After half a day skulking through
woodland and along hedgerows, accompanied
by three men from Levens who were sent to
guide us along the first part of the route, part
of our plan was presented to us. Duncan had
already suggested that being disguised as
Roundheads might give us our best chance
and as luck had it we spotted a camp of
soldiers in the valley below the edge of the
wood we had travelled through. There were
ten of them sitting around a fire while resting
their horses and cooking up a meal. We could
not see any others on guard duty and they

must have felt safe from intrusion. Their muskets were stacked in two stands and their horses were grazing in the field between us and the soldiers.

'If we can move along that hedgerow unnoticed we can catch them by surprise and it looks as though they are camped for the night so we could either wait until early morning or maybe this evening just as it gets dark.'

We all agreed we had more chance of catching them unawares first thing in the morning and as dawn was early at this time of year we would not be wasting too much time. Leaving Sam and Joe as lookouts the rest of our party backed off into the wood to rest and prepare for the morning. After clustering together around Duncan he explained the plan and while it was still light we checked our weapons and settled down with the cold food we had brought from the inn. Luke and I relieved Sam and Joe in the middle of the night and Duncan and the three Levens' men took the last watch. I was woken well before dawn and we quietly slid out of the trees and slowly crawled the hundred metres down towards the soldiers' camp. While on watch it had been noticed that two guards had been posted but not on our side of the camp. Duncan had sent the three Levens' men to deal with them and he was sure they would already be in place ready to jump them as soon as we attacked. Crawling on hands and knees for thirty minutes might have been something I found fun a few years ago but this was a hot, tiring and pretty painful experience and I was concentrating so much I bumped into the back of Luke who had stopped on Duncan's signalled orders. He looked around and gave me one of those looks only a mother or best friend can give and indicated we were level with the camp. The gate through the hedge gave us a quick and easy way into the camp, and from which there was no movement or sound as we clambered over it.

As per orders we created a half circle around the sleeping men and the cocking of five muskets immediately brought a reaction.

Duncan shouted orders aggressively at the men who lay on the ground with only one man swearing at us needing to be persuaded to be quiet by the end of Sam's boot. The Levens' men brought in the two guards although one; obviously the worse for wear, staggered and fell amongst the others holding his bloody jaw.

We quickly tied the men up with belts and ropes found in the camp and sat the sorry bunch back to back in pairs. Sam's rapid retribution seemed to keep the men quiet and two by two we stripped the men of their leather tunics and collected their helmets and weapons. Amongst the group was one civilian and the papers found on the troop leader explained his presence. Their horses were tacked and led into the camp, which we cleared of any evidence. It was decided the three Levens' men would take the men back as prisoners and after tying the men together in a chain gang strung behind one of their horses the men wished us well and moved off into the wood where we had previously hidden.

Naively I pointed out to Luke that I thought they would find it almost impossible to retrace our steps to Levens Hall with such a cargo.

'I am sure you are right Sol and I think the horses are of more value than the soldiers and if any of the Parliamentarians get back alive to the Hall I would be very surprised.'

Despite all the things I had seen during this war the cold murder of men who were not even given a chance to defend themselves filled me with horror but at the same time I realised that if these men escaped our lives would be short lived. I tried to push their faces out of my thoughts and now dressed in full Parliamentary gear I mounted my horse and fell in beside Luke as we trotted down the path away from the camp.

Duncan had questioned the men before they left and although some were reluctant to speak, others, hoping that by co-operating, their lives might be saved, had explained where they had come from and what their purpose had been. Papers from their sergeant showed they were telling the truth about their orders and Duncan pointed out that we needed to smarten up and behave like a proper cavalry troop.

We entered Lancaster having been stopped twice along the road and once on the outskirts of the town but our story and paperwork were obviously convincing. The task of the troop we were impersonating was to escort a gunsmith to Birmingham where arms were being manufactured for the Parliamentarians.

Joe was suitably dressed as the gunsmith and being a blacksmith he was well versed in the appropriate language. The specific reason for this gunsmith, it seemed from the paperwork, was the further development of the flintlock musket, which people were saying, would take over from the matchlock that most soldiers of the day were using. Seemingly a person of some import Joe hammed it up exceedingly, much to our annoyance, although this came in very handy when we were told to report to the town command post. Here we were asked for our papers and we introduced the important Joe who blinded the command post officer with the mechanics of the new weapon. We passed the inspection and went quickly to the gatehouse to check out the situation. The inn opposite the prison seemed a good starting place to find out information and sure enough some of the prison guards were taking refreshment. We made conversation and plied them with compliments and drink which resulted in them revealing that my brother was in fact in the gatehouse.

'Being moved tomorrow he is and we won't be sorry to see him go. Keeps making demands on us which although he pays well it always seems to mean us fetching and carrying.'

'Fetching and carrying what?' I said.

'Mostly food and sometimes clothes, I think he gives most of it away to the other prisoners.'

'Why move a prisoner from your establishment?' I asked the jailer.

'Well we are really only a debtors' prison and this one is to be tried for treason. They are moving him to Manchester tomorrow so perhaps we can get a bit of peace from then on.'

We stayed for a while before eventually moving out to sleep in the stables with our mounts.

'We should get up early and find a place along the Manchester road where we can intercept the prison party,' Duncan suggested.

'I know of a good place not far out of town where the road passes over a bridge in a fairly isolated position,' interjected Sam.

We agreed this was a suitable plan and at first light we rode out of the town along the road south. After an hour we came to the bridge, which had no settlement nearby in a valley with well-wooded slopes. We crossed the bridge and went up into the wood until we found a fairly level area to rest the horses and look back across the river.

Surveying the situation I suggested we find a tree we could place across the track near the bridge so that the prison guards would have to stop. We agreed this was a good plan and Duncan sent Sam and Joe off back down the road as lookouts. They crossed the bridge and after riding about a hundred yards down the road climbed into the wood. We could still see them and they were instructed to signal to us if the patrol was on its way by waving two white shirts or one shirt if it was not the prison guard but some other travellers.

The two-shirt wave triggered our action to drag the tree across the road and then take up our hidden positions around the bridge. From my position I could see the prison wagon being pulled by two horses with a driver and guard. Trotting behind the wagon were two cavalrymen who overtook the vehicle, which slowed as it approached the fallen tree. They looked around before dismounting, tying their mounts to the wagon and walking across the bridge to unblock the road. This was our best chance as the cavalrymen had left their carbines with their horses and only the wagon guard had his weapon at the ready. Duncan was the first to show himself and shout at the guard to drop his weapon. Startled by the sudden attack the guard brought his gun up to shoot and was shot in the chest by Duncan who jumped onto the road and threatened the driver. The two cavalrymen drew their swords but stopped in their tracks as Luke and I threatened them with our muskets. Sam and Joe soon arrived and they dragged the driver off the wagon and helped disarm the cavalrymen. Duncan and I opened the blacked out wagon with the driver's keys and much to our relief the only shackled figure in the wagon was Tom.

Even Tom was short of a quip as he climbed down from the back of the wagon and just hugged me before ruggedly shaking Duncan's hand.

'We must move quickly Tom,' said Duncan who then instructed that all the Parliamentarians should be searched and then locked in the wagon. This was done in a few minutes without much belligerence, as these men were fearful for their lives. Luke drove the wagon back along the road to the woodland entrance we had seen earlier and then deep into the undergrowth before we unhitched the horses.

We quickly discussed our situation with Tom who immediately took charge of our decision-making.

'We could try to get to Carlisle,' I suggested, but although we were all disguised we now had no relevant paperwork, which would give us a reason for going in that direction.

We were lucky that Joe knew this area well and he suggested that if we struck out eastward there were few settlements and the hills and dales would give us a good chance of not being seen if we were careful. This would be a long way round and would add days to our journey, but safety was more important than speed now we had successfully rescued Tom.

'I need to try and join up with Prince Rupert,' stated Tom. 'I heard while in prison that he had withdrawn from York after the Battle of Marston Moor and had gone back to Chester.'

'To get to Chester we would have to pass through Roundhead territory and that could be difficult,' interjected Joe.

After some thought Sam pointed out that we were close to the coast and perhaps we could go west to Poolton on the Wyre where he knew a number of fishermen.

'We could either borrow a boat or ask a skipper to take us south to Chester which would certainly be quicker than going north to Carlisle,' he added.

It was agreed that with Sam's nautical knowledge the sea route seemed the best option although Luke looked rather forlorn at the thought of another sea journey.

The weather was dry and warm and both men and horses were glad of the rest and the drink when we found an isolated valley, which contained a thirst quenching cool, tumbling stream. We settled down to eat and allow the horses to graze as the darkness fell and Tom was the first to speak as he made his way around all the men and thanked them individually for saving him. I could see by his manner why men admired him as a leader and eventually he sat down next to me.

'You will have to tell me what you have been up to Sol but first I must thank you for saving my life, I really could not see a way of beating the noose. The guards were saying I was to be tried in a few days and in my position I doubt if I would have been exchanged or ransomed.'

Over the next few hours I recounted the events of the past few months without holding back on my feelings for Rebecca but rather downplaying my relationship with Betsy. He listened attentively and only interrupted a few times when I could see he had his soldier's hat on as well as his brother's.

'You have done well Sol and you are a credit to Father who I am sure will be proud of the young man you have become.'

'When is this all going to end Tom, we seem to be going round in circles and Luke and I now have no real plan for the future?'

'When we get to Chester things may be a little clearer but I think you should consider joining our forces if you think the King's stand is the right one, I obviously do but I am not trying to sway your views other than saying I think you are going to have to choose sides.'

'I have never thought of any other way than to support the King. To me it seems the right thing to do but perhaps, as you say, things may be clearer when we reach Chester.'

'We should get some sleep Sol, the next few days are going to be dangerous and difficult but from what you have told me you seem to be used to hardship and adventure.'

The next day we moved westwards guided by Sam's navigation which turned out to be assisted by a piece of equipment he held in a leather pouch.

'I was given this compass by Prince Rupert after our swimming expedition and it should help prevent us going round in circles even if we travel at night,' he explained.

He showed me the instrument with pride and over the next few days started to explain to me how sailors navigate. In the evenings he would draw lines and angles in the earth and point out useful stars as he explained the method he used as a sailing master. Although at first I found it completely bewildering I slowly started to pick up the technique and the related mathematics. I have, since those days, always been fascinated by navigation and during this learning period I had no idea how useful this information would be to me in the future.

It only took us two days and nights to reach the river and the coast where Sam led us to a cottage set away from the village. It was dark when we arrived hungry and tired.

'Best if you all stay back here in the wood while I go to the cottage. I know the family and they will welcome me but I must check to see what they think about half the Royalist Army coming to dinner.'

About an hour later Sam returned with news and an invitation to use the barn as all the animals had been turned out into the fields.

'John Dunne is the farmer and like most farmers around here he also does some fishing, along with his brother. He said the locals were divided in their allegiances but as far as he could tell no one had caused anyone else any real trouble. Generally people were trying to keep a low profile and most hoped the whole war would pass them by although the news of Royalist Press Gangs has frightened everyone.'

We trotted down to the barn, fed and watered the horses before John Dunne came out with a piping hot pot of stew and a flagon of ale. We all thanked him heartily and he sat down with us on a bale of straw.

'You will need to leave as soon as possible as we never know when a patrol may come through. It has been quiet recently but I am not sure if that is good or bad news. Sam said a boat is required for you and your horses, which under normal circumstances would be out of the question as our fishing boats are far too small to accommodate large animals. However, as luck would have it, there is a boat that you might be able to use. A while back some Royalists tried to negotiate the estuary and got stuck, we helped them ashore and they abandoned the boat. It has taken us some time to retrieve it from the muddy grip of the river but it is now fully seaworthy.

We took turns to watch for any unwelcome visitors by riding up to the wood and watching the road into the village. My watch was alongside Sam who, as the sun started to rise above the horizon, told me some of what to expect regarding the ship in the estuary and our future voyage.

'It seems the boat is a small merchant ship which between us we should be able to handle as long as the weather stays favourable. We will have to take it well out in the bay before returning south to Chester. This should help us avoid suspicion and also keep us away from the lee shore with winds from the west and south west.'

'How long should the journey be Sam?' I asked.

'Probably today and most of tomorrow, depending how far west we go, but we should certainly hope to be in Chester in three days.'

In the morning we took our horses down to the dock and hauled them aboard using a sling and tackle with the help of John and other fishermen. They were shackled below and given straw and water to calm them. We set about learning what we needed to do to sail the craft under Sam's instructions and four of the local fishermen volunteered to go with us as they said they could return with the fishermen who took fish into Chester. The vessel was a small three-masted merchant ship, which probably belonged to the Royalists who had abandoned it. We would be returning it, possibly to its owners, although the fishermen were hoping for a reward, a suggestion that Tom said he would support when he arrived in Chester. We were assigned jobs, which were supervised by the fishermen and Sam who took over the steering mechanism. It was decided we should leave immediately as the tide and wind were mostly in our favour and the prospect of crewing such a large vessel was creating an air of excitement in the group. Luke looked somewhat apprehensive but being on deck with a specific job to do seemed to stem the seasickness, which had previously hit him so hard.

The most difficult job for the crew would be having to reef or let loose the square rigged sails when only five of us had ever even climbed any rigging on a moving boat.

Sam decided that the four fishermen could unfurl enough sail on the main and foremasts with us pulling the appropriate rigging and once this was done we ran forward to help hoist two jib sails. We were mostly a bit short on our knowledge of sailing terminology and I recount this as I recall us gradually and literally learning the ropes.

The early morning offshore breeze took us quickly out of the estuary and well into the bay and with the sun shining brightly the day started well. The fishermen released enough sail for us to make what to me seemed rapid headway and we were all kept busy hauling and tightening various lines. I checked on the horses, which seemed to be coping well with the movement of the vessel. While below decks I explored the other compartments. There was a small captain's cabin, which had a cot, a desk attached to the wall and one chair. The crew must have slept in hammocks in the only section not taken up by the cargo and there was one small locked door which seemed to front a small room. I broke open the lock with a metal bar and with my lantern in hand I peered inside. This must have been the arms and powder store so I backed out quickly and hung my lantern on a hook, which hung from the beam behind me. The light was good enough for me to make out at least twenty muskets, some pistols hanging in racks and a number of small barrels, which on closer inspection had either 'powder' or 'shot,' stamped on the top. I closed and locked the door as best I could and went back on deck where I informed Tom of my find.

'I expect when they got stuck in the river they were unable to take all their weapons when the fishermen rescued them,' suggested Tom.

'Take Duncan down and ask him to inspect them to see if they will be of any use if we need them.'

Duncan and I spent some time checking the firearms and he felt the powder was dry and of a good quality. We also found some barrels of tar and some timber, which were probably part of a previous cargo crammed into the forward hold.

The whole of the day was then spent keeping the sails trimmed and Sam explained to me how to steer the boat taking compass bearings and sail trim into consideration. I took over the wheel while he rested and planned out our route. The fishermen helped Sam check our speed with a knotted line and he plotted our position on a chart found in the cabin. He estimated we were now around forty miles west of our origin and just as night fell we changed to a due south course from our previous westerly route. With the gentle wind from the south west we did not find the night travel difficult and the crew were split into three watches with two always on deck and one man stationed well forward to look out for lights of other vessels although we were not showing any navigation lights.

It was first light, which brought the shock.

'Sail off the port bow,' shouted one of the fishermen.

We all crowded over to the side of the boat and could clearly see a boat of similar size to us some distances away. Judging distance at sea is an art gained through experience and those in the know soon agreed it was about two miles away and although we had the advantage of the windward side of the breeze Sam was not confident we could out run them.

'They already have full sail and have obviously spotted us. It looks like a small armed brig which means cannon and we will soon be in range.'

'It must be Roundhead navy by the look of the flags,' interjected Joe.

'We don't look armed, they must think we are merchants but perhaps we can give them a bit of a shock,' said Tom.

We all turned to Tom and he must have noticed our looks of disbelief when a sudden thump from cannon made us all instinctively look back at the brig. A waterspout exploded around thirty yards in front of us followed by another thump. I did not see where the next shot fell as Tom quickly regained our attention.

'How long before they reach us?' asked Tom.

'Perhaps an hour, although as you can see we are almost in cannon range,' answered Sam.

'Right this is what we do,' said Tom who was now obviously in charge of the situation.

'Duncan, take Luke and Joe and bring up all the muskets load them and position them on the deck on the port side. Solomon, collect your bow and make fire arrows and bring up a barrel of tar.'

He then instructed two of the fishermen to start reefing in the sails and Sam was already lowering the flag we trailed at our stern. The other two fishermen he set about launching the small sailing skiff on the starboard side out of view from the enemy. The others started bringing up the barrels of shot and powder and loading them into the skiff. Just for good measure they also emptied a barrel of tar into the hull of the small craft.

'We must look as though we are helpless and quite happy to be boarded,' said Tom.

'When close enough we will then sail the skiff around the stern and into the side of the brig. Solomon will set the skiff alight as it hits the brig's side and we must continue the surprise by firing as many muskets at them as we can.'

'There are at least three loaded muskets each,' interjected Duncan.

Tom gave all his instructions without the slightest hint that we might fail despite the fact that this was a preposterous plan to attempt against a well-armed brig.

'I will sail the skiff,' said Tom.

'Wait a minute,' responded Sam; 'I think that's a job for a sailor.'

Sam took control and asked two fishermen to collect as much light rope they could and put it in the skiff. He then tied the end to the stern rail and explained.

'I will tie this around my waist and jump from the skiff when it is in position and I would be grateful if you could haul me aboard when you have dealt with the brig.'

We all looked at Sam with disbelief but he quickly responded with a smile and a shake of his head. We laughed more in nervousness than hilarity at the situation and then all ran to our positions.

One of the fishermen took the wheel but as we only had the minimum of sail his job was to keep us parallel to the brig.

He did this to perfection and the rest of us lined the port side and waved to the sailors on the brig. Some waved back and they seemed unprepared for any retaliation from us, which was not surprising as they had their guns run out and we were seemingly unarmed.

I had prepared my fire arrows, which were hidden, with my bow on the deck and my job was to fire the skiff at just the right time. The distance I estimated would be less than fifty yards and the wind was light and in my favour. I felt confident that I could hit the target but was doubtful of the consequences.

A shout from the brig warned us that we were to be boarded in the name of the Parliamentary cause. Tom shouted a reply to say we were bringing goods from Lancashire to the south and that we were happy to accommodate them.

We were no more than fifty yards apart when the skiff suddenly appeared around the stern of our boat and headed for the brig.

'What is the meaning of this,' shouted the master of the brig.

'We thought your men would like a taste of our barrelled wares Sir,' Tom replied.

The hesitation created just enough time for the skiff to bump into the side of the brig and Sam could be seen throwing a grappling line onto the brig's side and then, much to the enemy sailors' surprise, he jumped into the water.

I let loose four fire arrows in a few seconds and everyone hit the target just as our men lining the side ripped a volley of fire into the sailors lining the brig's side. The explosion was far greater than I ever expected and knocked me backwards as a huge sheet of flame enveloped the whole side of the brig. One more volley of musket fire was followed by our fishermen scrambling into the rigging and unfurling the sheets. We seemed to lurch forward as the wind took hold and we rapidly drew away from the brig, which in the confusion had not fired a single shot in retaliation. The flames had leaped into the rigging and sails of the brig and as some of the acrid smoke cleared we could see the panic on board as men rushed to try and stem the fires. Luke and I ran to the stern and started hauling at the line Sam had tied to himself and it was much to everyone's relief that an exhausted and thoroughly waterlogged Sam was finally pulled up through the stern window into the cabin.

We left the smoking brig behind as we sailed south and as the evening approached we could more easily see land to our east and ahead of us.

'The mouth of the Dee is only a few miles ahead and the tide is right for us to sail into Chester,' said Sam.

A Royalist gunboat rowed its way out to meet us and then escort us back towards Chester where we anchored in the river's deep central channel.

It was dark as we were rowed to the dock but Tom was instantly recognised by the Major in charge of the port area. He then provided us with an escort and told us to report to the command post of Prince Rupert which was still in the tavern we had visited before. Tom was received and invited to explain our presence while the rest of us were fed and watered in the section of the tavern not used by the officers. Some of the officers came through to find out our story and the rank barriers were surprisingly quickly lowered after a few rounds of drinks.

Tom emerged with a pouch, which he presented to the fishermen as reward for the return of the merchant ship. They were delighted and we bade them farewell as they wished to seek out some fishermen who would aid their return to the village.

'You all get some rest,' said Tom, 'and we will discuss the future in the morning. It looks as though the Prince may have a proposition for you to consider.'

The next morning I was woken by Tom with the worst possible news.

'It seems that the boat taking Rebecca to France never reached its destination. A storm had hit the Bay of Biscay and it is supposed the boat sank as no survivors have been reported.'

Tom stayed with me as I asked questions I knew he could not answer and the grief suddenly hit me and that I would never see Rebecca again. Our time together had been so brief and her death seemed such a waste.

Tom must have told Luke who kept me company for a while but for the next three days I was virtually inconsolable. Eventually I regained some strength mostly from the friends around and I decided to seek out Betsy.

The inn where Betsy had gained a job when I last saw her was busy and noisy but welcoming. I bought an ale and asked for Betsy. The barman sent a boy out through the bar and after a few moments Betsy appeared.

She looked as I had never seen her before, well dressed, clean and tidy. She rushed across the room and hugged me to the amusement of the men surrounding us. There was a tear in her eyes as she pulled me into an adjoining empty room.

'Sol, I never thought I would see you again, what are you doing back here?'

I retold my tale and she cried when I told her about Rebecca but laughed at the incident with the brig. I lost track of time but as I ended my story the inn had become quiet and the drinking time was over.

'I suppose I should return to my lodgings,' I said.

Betsy hugged and kissed me and led me through to what were her quarters.

'Do you live here Betsy?' I asked.

'I should think the owner of an inn should live in it, wouldn't you?'

'You are the owner?' I said in a startled voice, which brought a rather black look from Betsy.

'Yes. Your money and my luck made it possible for me to buy the place. As the previous owner was in debt, I paid the debt in return for the inn and since then I have already recouped my investment.'

I stayed the night and we made love. My emotions were a confusing mixture of thoughts of Rebecca and a real affection for Betsy. Could a man love two so seemingly different women? Could I ever love Betsy as I thought I could have loved Rebecca? Why did I always long to see Betsy whenever she was near?

'Don't do too much thinking Sol,' said Betsy obviously seeing confusion in my face. 'These are strange times and we must make the best of the time we have. You are the only man who has ever shown me respect and affection and I love you for it, but let's not think too far ahead as everything is so uncertain.'

'You found Betsy then,' observed Luke as I walked into our lodgings the next morning.

I did not have to explain but I retold Betsy's story and Luke who also liked Betsy a great deal was pleased she had done so well.

'Tom wants us to meet him in an hour at the command post along with Duncan and the lads. It seems he has some news for us.'

The news was both astonishing and to a certain extent flattering.

'As you know,' Tom started, once we had all gathered at the tavern, 'Sam and Joe are agents for Prince Rupert. They have now been assigned a task, which requires much daring and travelling. They require assistance and have already recruited Duncan and hoped very much that you two would join them.'

'Tom, Luke and I are now fully committed to the King's cause and would be proud to help Sam and Joe if we can,' I looked at Luke who nodded.

'The task is for you to go to Scotland and liaise with the Marquess of Montrose who has now taken the side of the King and is about to confront the Covenanters near to Perth. He hopes to take control of the town where we have reason to believe a horde of treasure, collected by the clans for the Parliamentary cause, is being held. We want you to accompany The Marquess into the town and relieve them of the horde.'

'Then we go to The Netherlands,' interrupted a voice with a foreign accent.

'Captain Lopez, it's good to see you, but where do you fit into this plan?' I asked as we shook hands.

'We are to take the horde to The Netherlands where a friend of the King has organised for a large contingent of mercenaries to return with us to fight for the King's cause. It will be my responsibility to command the mercenaries and the horde is the war chest for paying their wages and purchasing passage and some equipment.'

'The details and letters from the Prince are with the Captain and preparations have been made so that you can sail with the morning tide. Duncan will take command of the operation and Captain Lopez will run the negotiations in the Netherlands. You will however be under the ultimate command of the Marquess while in Scotland,' added Tom.

'You are not going with us then Tom?' I asked.

'No Sol, my place is on the battlefield with The Prince but I know you are in good hands and you can obviously look after yourself. You are the best men for the job and I have been proud to fight with you all.' Tom shook everyone by the hand and then ushered me to one side.

'This is an important and dangerous task Sol and I am not sure that your mission is as secret as we would have liked. It seems that someone has leaked information about the horde and therefore you might not be the only group looking for it.'

'Do you have any idea who it could be?' I asked.

'I have no proof but if you come across Caxton be on your guard.'

'Caxton, I thought he was on The Isle of Man.'

'Things change quickly Sol and it seems he came back to Chester when the Earl left the island. Prince Rupert has sent him to Scotland with a hundred cavalry to support. The Marquess but I have some information, which leads me to believe he knows about the horde. He will have travelled from Carlisle to Edinburgh whereas you will be taking a boat to Ayr and then travelling north east to meet up with The Marquess. You should arrive around the same time and I hope in time to join The Marquess in his attempt to take Perth.

We sailed the next morning in a well-armed brig. This time we were just passengers, which was somewhat of a relief after our recent escapades. I had again spent the night with Betsy and we held each other close, as we both knew our futures were uncertain. I felt Betsy's tears on my shoulder and I kissed her face.

'I have not cried since I was a child Solomon, I am sorry I know there cannot be a future for us but you are the first man I have felt like this with and I am not sure how to react.' With this she passed me a small cloth rapped parcel.

'Take this, I hope it helps you find me again one day but do not open it now.'

'I hope to see you again when this is all over Betsy but you must get on with your life. Your business is doing well and although the outcome of the war is uncertain you should be safe. All soldiers love a tavern whichever side they fight for.'

As we sailed along the coast I thought of Betsy, what she had said and the present she had given me. It was still in my pocket and enclosed in the thick cloth was a handsome pocket compass. This was obviously a rare and expensive item and I wondered how Betsy had come by such a sought after instrument. I was determined to return one day to see the woman who I now realised was not only my lover but also a good friend. It was another good friend who patted me on the shoulder and spoke as I turned my attention away from the sea.

'A penny for your thoughts then Solomon,' said Luke who looking into my face continued; 'no need to say anything. She is a fine woman Solomon and any man should be proud to have her as a friend.'

'Thanks Luke, she is indeed a remarkable woman and I just fear for her safety if things go against us in Chester.'

Luke did not reply which indicated he also was thinking along the same lines, but did say that Duncan wanted to see us all in the wardroom to discuss the mission.

The Captain of the brig vacated his cabin and the marines were removed from outside the door for our meeting with Duncan. Luke and I sat on the bench with the stern window at our backs and Sam, Joe and Captain Lopez squeezed in around the desk. Duncan sat in the captain's chair with a number of charts laid out before him on the desk. It always amazed me at the lack of space on a warship. The ceiling beams were so low I could never stand up straight and even the captain's quarters were a simple, small room with a cot, a desk, a few chairs and a trunk. I had been below decks and the sixty sailors and marines were simply squashed in amongst the requirements of war.

Duncan pointed to a map as he outlined our route.

'We should arrive in Ayr tomorrow evening and we are sure the clans in the area between the coast and Perth are Royalist supporters and we should have no trouble getting their permission to pass through their lands. However we must be vigilant at all times and be prepared for the unexpected. When we reach Perth I will report to The Marquess who will issue us with orders until the horde is found. Once that is secure, a boat awaits us on the east coast and from there we sail to The Netherlands. As you know we are to pick up a cargo of mercenaries and weapons and sail back to Bristol: any questions?'

Duncan was right. We had little trouble travelling through the central part of Scotland through Glasgow and on to Stirling and eventually meeting up with the Marquess who was now camped with his army at Tippermuir.

Duncan reported to the Marquess who asked if we would be part of the army about to take Perth. Duncan said we should be allocated where we would be most useful.

Duncan and I were assigned to the archery unit and their minders whilst Luke, Sam and Joe were given muskets and joined a troop of musketeers. Captain Lopez was to remain with the Marquess and his personal guard.

On receiving our orders we were also given passes which meant that we could leave our groups when we reached Perth so that we could pursue our mission without being shot for desertion.

'When we get to Perth we must try to get together as quickly as possible. There is likely to be complete chaos if the town is taken by force so watch your backs and stick together. We will try to meet outside the Cathedral as we believe the horde to be in the vault below the treasury house nearby. We have been assigned a tent but we must be ready for a call to action at any time so I suggest we see to the horses and then prepare ourselves for battle.' There was a general look of shock on some of our faces at the sound of the word 'battle' which was spotted by Duncan who laughed and then added; 'stay calm and watch out for each other. The Roundheads are mostly untrained young men who have never fired a shot in anger. The Scots are the ones to fear but they only outnumber us by about three to one, now let's see to the horses and get some food.'

It was a quiet evening under the stars, none of us spoke much and if anyone said anything I can't remember what it was. We were all thinking about tomorrow and our first involvement in a battle.

Chapter Seven

TIPPERMUIR
(September 1644)

I was about to loose an arrow at a man for the first time, which man I did not know but while waiting for the order to fire I knew this was most certainly different to killing a deer. I, an Englishman, surrounded by mostly Scots and Irish was about to fire at the mass of Scottish Clansmen who had gathered at Tippermuir. They obviously greatly outnumbered us, some were saying by five to one although those who said it seemed to take pride in the poor odds. Duncan to my right pointed out the mass of cavalry on either side of the foot troops.

'If they get close aim at the horses Solomon, but I doubt if they will.' I wanted to ask why he was so sure but shouts from the soldiers only around five hundred yards away broke through the general chatter.

'Jesus and no quarter,' they shouted repeatedly 'Jesus and no quarter.' Heart rates around me must have risen as angry oaths were thrown back at the enemy. The archers around me seemed unsettled as Duncan grabbed my arm.

'Look lad it's Montrose,' I followed his pointing of his bow to see the man we followed, the friend of my father and the reason I was now standing in the middle of a Scottish valley; James Graham, First Marquess of Montrose.

Montrose rode from in front of the Irish troops who were in the centre of our assembly and the chatter subsided as we all watched his movements. His green and black sash stood out over his highly polished armour and he took off his plumed helmet and turned towards us.

'I will send The Master of Madertie to Lord Elcho to ask for his surrender or see if he wishes to fight tomorrow and not on the Sabbath. I doubt if he has the wit to take his chance to withdraw now and expect him to believe he's doing God's work and therefore will feel the Sabbath is appropriate.

Gentlemen, it is true you have few arms; your enemy, however, to all appearance, have plenty. My advice to you is therefore, as there happens to be a great abundance of stones on this moor, every man should provide himself, in the first place with as stout a one as he can manage, rush up to the first Covenanter he meets, beat out his brains, take his sword and I believe they will be at no loss as how to proceed, they will run.'

The men as one gave out a great roar that seemed a mixture of laughter and anger. I just cheered. I wasn't sure why, as the contents of Montrose's speech seemed to highlight our predicament, but I must admit to a feeling of excitement taking over from fear.

Montrose swung around, waved to some cavalry to his right and a sole horseman rode out across the moor towards Elcho's army He was clutching a lance with a white flag of truce attached and streaming out behind him. Three riders rode to meet him. At first both armies cheered but as the horsemen met, a tense quiet descended on the whole gathering. They exchanged greetings and talked for some minutes and although I was completely absorbed by the event I did notice a large number of people moving over the hill behind the enemy with some settling down on the grass. For a moment I thought these were reinforcing Elcho's already large army but it soon became obvious these were local people, men, women and children who had come to watch the battle.

'Have you noticed the observers Solomon?' said Duncan. 'The good Burgers of Perth must think this is going to be a quick and easy win.'

Then the one thing no one expected happened. The three Elcho horsemen attacked Madertie and forced him back to the baying ranks of their men. Elcho's cavalry then suddenly charged towards our group of archers and axe men. I had obviously never seen axe men fight cavalry but these experienced fighters ran out in groups of four and stood ahead of the front row of archers. Lord Kilpoint the leader of our group shouted loudly and calmly.

'On my order fire a volley at the riders, then in your own time bring down the horses.'

I could hit a moving deer at two hundred yards, a stationary one at three hundred yards. Could I hit a man on a horse riding towards me who wants to run me through and trample me into the mud of the moor? The cavalry of more than one hundred horses was around three hundred yards away and moving fast, the ground started to tremble under the weight and sound, of this mass of horseflesh men and armour.

'Make the first one count Solomon,' said Duncan. Select your rider; forget the rest. After that, aim at the horse's throat above the protected chest.'

My bow was strung, my heavy tipped arrow was nocked, my spare bowstrings lay dry under my hat and a quiver of arrows at my side. Four arrows were stuck in the earth in front of me and I was as ready as I could be but could I hit a man and stand whilst being charged? The 'get ready' order came to jolt me out of my thoughts. I picked my target and on Kilpoint's shout I shot. I watched to see if I could trace my shot but Duncan quietly said: 'just shoot boy, don't' count hits.' The first volley lashed into the front thirty to forty riders and men and horses went down like a wave, bringing down some closely following gallopers. I loosed my four arrows from the turf within a few seconds (I can normally shoot around 14 in a minute, which is as many as anyone I know). More horsemen fell now only forty paces from our line, which is when the axe men rose up and charged. It seemed wildly at first but these men fought in well-organised small groups bringing down horses and men while being protected by others in the group. One large longhaired axe man caught my eye as he stood his ground waiting for a horse. Around him his three protectors fought off the sideswipes of cavalrymen. He then stepped forward into the path of a well armoured charging horse and brought it crashing to the ground with a full swing of his axe. The others quickly killed the rider and then regained their positions for the next horse. The archers were killing horses, which were milling around in the chaos and within a few minutes those that were able were racing back to Elcho's lines.

The retreating horsemen scattered Elcho's line of infantry and seeing this Montrose charged his cavalry into the chaos.

'Archers forward,' shouted Kilpoint and we trotted after him and his personal guards. The ground was firm and we soon came within striking distance of the confused opposition.

'Stand,' shouted Kilpoint. 'Hit the musketeers.'

We fired in our own time from a distance less than 100 yards. We could not miss. A few muskets went off as we could see the Irish marching in a well discipline line towards the central set of Elcho's troops who had raised their muskets. I watched as the Irish seemingly well ordered approached, stopped not one hundred yards away and with a deafening crash opened fire. Elcho's troops seemed to fall or freeze as the Irish with a great howl threw themselves at their foe. It was said there were nine cannons against us but I heard no explosion and the Covenanters who manned the cannon turned and fled.

Our infantry and cavalry were now fully involved in hand to hand fighting but it was the ferocity of our clansmen, partly armed with stones, which seemed to unnerve Elcho's men. With most of the opposition in full, disorganised retreat we were ordered to direct our aim at a group who were making a stand around a few farm cottages. Their resistance did not last long and the whole battle seemed to be running away from us. Our archers had now broken ranks and were joining in the chase.

'Watch out for the injured; they are still dangerous,' shouted Duncan, who then bent over and removed a gold band from a cavalryman's arm. There were dead and dying horses scattered over the field alongside their riders who as far as I could see were all dead. For a moment I stood still and looked around me. There were other archers simply standing and watching, while others were looting the dead. We were well behind the main retreating battle now, which seemed to be moving through the group of townsfolk who had watched from the hill. Kilpoint started to issue orders through his sergeants and we gathered together as a group and set off at a trot down the road after the retreating horde. The carnage around us was unbelievable and there was little sign of life from the men we passed. Kilpoint was just a few yards ahead of me when a seemingly dead musketeer rose up in front of us. I shot him in the throat and his gun went off harmlessly. Kilpoint turned and touched his cap in acknowledgment.

'Well done laddie,' said Duncan. 'If we live through this, that action could take you far.'

Not really sure what he meant I trotted on, now fully alert to the dangers of the battlefield and for the next two hours we followed the retreat.

We entered Perth, which was abandoned by the soldiers, but the local people in fear of their lives had mostly locked themselves in their homes. We could see our officers confronting what seemed like the city elders who were obviously trying to ensure the safety of the citizens and their possessions. Our troops were surprisingly calm, now that the opposition had fled and being chased by the cavalry, so their officers took it upon themselves to find food and drink for their men. Gradually the populace appeared and were quick to provide for the occupying force.

'Let's go to the Cathedral, 'said Duncan.

We had not seen any of our group during the fighting and it was with trepidation that I approached the church. I need not have worried as Luke, Sam and Joe were all sitting on the steps waiting for us.

After a brief but emotional set of greetings Duncan pointed out the treasury house a hundred yards down the road.

'Make sure you are loaded and ready,' he said.

We trotted down the road to find the door broken and two surprised cavalrymen inside. They drew their swords and ordered us outside. We ignored their protestations and with muskets levelled at them they dropped their weapons.

'Keep an eye on them,' Duncan ordered Sam and Joe.

The rest of us slowly crept along the passageway and checked the rooms as we passed. There was no one to be seen, although a light could be seen moving at the bottom of the stairs to the cellar. Duncan went first with Luke and I following close behind.

'Thanks for finding the Prince's horde Caxton,' Duncan said to the man whose back was towards us. He turned with pistol in hand which he fired catching Duncan in the shoulder. He went down with a crash and Caxton stood brandishing his sword in front of us and we clashed swords as I tried to draw him away from Duncan.

'You again, you brat, it's about time someone taught you some manners.'

We clashed again but the lack of room meant this soon turned into a brawl and we fell together over some furniture and he quickly regained his footing to stand over me. I stabbed him in the leg with the knife I always kept in by boot and he backed off cursing and limping straight into Luke who unceremoniously bashed him on the head with his musket stock. I crawled over to Duncan who seemed to have partially recovered. He saw the look on my face and tried to assure me he was fine and that it was only a flesh wound.

'Get the chests lads, while I see to his lordship here,' said Duncan who, with obvious difficulty, started tying Caxton to a pillar.

Sam and Joe arrived to tell us the cavalrymen had been taken care of and helped us with the two chests full of gold pieces and various valuable trinkets. As had been arranged we emerged from the house to be met by Captain Lopez who had arrived with a bodyguard of cavalry and a cart whereupon we loaded the chests and made our way to Melrose's main camp.

The camp adjutant allocated us an area sealed off from the main camp by our troop of cavalry and we all gathered in the large tent with the horde in the two chests. Duncan had his shoulder treated by two women who revealed that the ball had clipped his shoulder, which had bled well and was clean. They bandaged him and offered him a sling, which he refused with a withering glance.

'Got work to do lassie, but thanks all the same, I will need the use of both arms for where we're off to.'

We had all survived the battle without many physical signs but the look on the faces of all the men surrounding me made me realise how lucky we had been. We were now off on another major adventure as it happens on a captured pirate vessel from Dundee to Europe.

At this time I did not realise the significance of the vessel but that was to become clear in the months to come. We sailed at the end of September and as the coast slipped away I wondered how long it would be before I might see England or even Betsy again. I surprised myself with my regrets at leaving her and vowed to make her a priority when we returned.

Chapter Eight

THE BLOND ARAB

Jan Janszoon stood on the cliff top overlooking the Bristol Channel and took a deep breath as he reflected on his adventure packed life. Until three years ago he had spent most of his adult life as a highly successful pirate using various staging posts in North Africa. He had recently spent time in his Moorish castle with his daughter Lysbeth but she had now returned to The Netherlands and they both knew they had said their last farewells. He had grown bored with the last few indolent years and had returned to his great love of sailing and piracy and even at the venerable age of sixty-nine he was determined not to die in his bed. Not that he had a death wish, just that he wanted to experience the thrill of the chase for as long as possible.

The cliff was on the Isle of Lundy and although Murat Rais, as he was generally known to his Muslim compatriots, was used to all weathers he was pleasantly surprised by the warmth of the South Westerly that gently blew across the small island.

He was also surprised by the way the English seemed to ignore the presence of the Arab pirate colony that had sprung up over the last couple of years although he felt that once the English Civil War was over the government would probably pay them a little more attention.

Looking along the coast he could see his fleet of six boats riding the gentle swell in the lee of the island. Behind him the sight of the Islamic flag fluttering in the breeze on Marisco Castle's battlements brought a smile to his face. The conditions were good for the expedition in which they were about to partake and although he was confident of success and excited about the prospect of attaining an English treasure he was also apprehensive about taking on the English ships in their own waters.

The intelligence he had received made it clear that a single brig with a schooner escort was to travel down the east coast of England with a horde of Celtic treasure on board bound for his old homeland of The Netherlands. He had calculated that his fleet should sail along the English Channel and then beat up the east coast in patrol order until they contacted the prize. He was now waiting for reports to come back to verify the situation.

A trumpet wailed a call to prayer from the battlements of the castle and Jan started back along the headland to his fortified home where he would join other pirates of the same faith in the Mecca directed ritual.

His pirate band of eight hundred 'lost souls' as he affectionately called them was made up of a motley mixture of races, creeds and class with even a number of elite Janissaries*.

Many of these men and indeed some of the women had served with him for a number of years and although the well established code of the corsairs meant that the crews could vote for their captain, in this instance no one was under any illusion as to who was in charge. Jan's followers had either joined via the press or voluntarily, but all were treated equally and they were now almost all equally well off.

As he approached the castle he stood for a moment to compare the defences with that of his most recent home in the fortress of Oualidia near Safi in Morocco. He had lived there for the past four years in some splendour and indolence as Governor but now he felt invigorated by the new challenges of, what he realised was likely to be, his last major foray before again returning to North Africa.

On entering the castle he was immediately joined by Asif, a Janissary, who for over twenty years had been at his side as advisor, bodyguard and most importantly his most loyal friend. Asif was a true warrior and even if he was now well past his prime he continued to be a formidable opponent in any physical challenge. Being well over six feet tall, broad shouldered and with a massive and slightly greying moustache he was certainly a sight to behold. His colourful attire and huge scimitar hanging loosely by his side gave him an air of authority and he was highly respected by all the crews, many who had seen him in fighting action noting how glad they were that he was on their side. He was nicknamed 'Viking' behind his back due to his strangely orange hair and light skin.

Without speaking, but with a reciprocated nod, the two men made their way to the small castle chapel. Jan had no qualms about facing Mecca and performing his Islamic rituals in a church built for Christians. Their short prayer session was interrupted by excited shouts from outside.

'Sounds as if we may have news Jan,' said Asif.

They left the chapel by the side door, which led into the main castle bailey, to be met by a crowd of noisy corsairs.

'Captain, the Falcon has returned with news of the English,' shouted one of the men.

'Where is Captain Allesandri?' asked Jan.

'Still down in the harbour, but news about the English was shouted down to the bum boats who passed it on to us,' replied the spokesman.

'Well I think we should find out the news from the horse's mouth rather than its arse,' shouted Jan with reference to the bum boats.

The men laughed as they accompanied their charismatic leader down the track to the dock where the Polacca* named The Falcon was anchored one hundred yards out into the harbour. Small boats were milling about her and Captain Allesandri could be seen standing regally in the stern of a cutter, which was making rapid progress towards the dock.

The September weather was calm and bright and the dashing boat with its resplendent skipper was a sight that brought a smile to the rugged face of the tall blond pirate leader. Jan walked down to the end of the dock to receive his friend and most able captain.

The pirates on the dock cheered as Allesandri leapt off the cutter to be immediately embraced by Jan. This comradeship was one of the main reasons Jan had returned to pirating having left the politicking to others back in Morocco.

The men also reacted well to the obvious trust and friendship of their leading captains and the throng soon turned into a celebration party once Jan had announced he had positive news of the English and that the pirate fleet would be leaving the next day.

The friendship between the Italian and the Dutch captain was a strange one considering their background but it was based on personal and not political, nor historic lines. Yes, Jan had been captured and tortured by Knights of Malta and yes, Allesandri had once been such a Knight, but all this counted for nothing after Allesandri had single-handedly saved Jan's daughter from the clutches of a cold and inhospitable sea many years ago. Allesandri had been a highly respected figure in the courts of Venice and Rome but a fight to the death with a minor royal had meant his having to leave his homeland for good. On leaving, the boat in which he was travelling had been attacked by Jan and his pirates and during the melee Allesandri had seen the young Lysbeth blown out of the rear window of his attacker's boat when a cannon had exploded. Seeing she was still alive he had jumped in and saved her life. He never expected to be treated as a hero by his enemies, for whom he now commanded a boat, but he was and he now thoroughly enjoyed the thrilling lifestyle he had literally fallen into and the friendship of his leader Jan Janszoon.

'You seem to have had a successful voyage my friend,' said Jan. 'We are all relieved to see you seemingly all intact.'

'Thank you Jan, yes we have returned without losing a spar or a man with what we think is sound information. As I have reported the English are moving down the East Coast of England. We intercepted some fishermen who had seen the brig and the schooner anchored up for the night on the previous day. We could have taken prisoners but they gave the information freely and they may be of use to us again.

Certainly word will now be getting around we are in their waters as some of the fishermen fled at the sight of us and retreated to their coves and inlets, but that could not be helped.'

'You have done well friend, now we must prepare our plan for tomorrow. We will eat together this evening with the other captains and I will explain my strategy. Having sailed the Channel and East Coast, which I have not, I value any information you can provide.'

The corsairs, hearing the news of the voyage on the morrow partied well and by the morning the rather bedraggled crews began to prepare to leave the island. One area of concern to Jan was the plight of the five hundred captured English he had acquired over the last few months from raids along the south west coast of England and the west coast of Ireland The English always brought a high price in the slave markets whereas he tried never to imprison any Celts who now thought of him as some kind of hero.

Some say his reasoning was that the light coloured skinned Celts often succumbed to the raging heat of North Africa whereas the darker skinned Europeans seemed to cope more easily, but he knew it was because of the hero worship he enjoyed at the expense of the surly English. It was a fact that he had never come across a more determined and aggressive foe. He had fought more ruthless and barbaric peoples but the English stood apart as formidable and belligerent opponents and with this in mind he made his plans carefully.

The island and prisoners were left with a guard of fifty men leaving over four hundred men to crew the five boats he had decided to take. As he and Asif looked across the harbour many small boats were carrying men and resources to the five largest vessels in the fleet. There were three Polaccas each with a crew of about seventy five and well armed with twenty four cannon of various sizes. The other two vessels were large Xebecs,* each containing 34 guns and crews upwards of one hundred men, one of which 'The Storm' was Jan's flagship while the other, 'The Tempest' was captained by Ahmed Hussein.

To his men Jan was thought of as a great leader who although generally fair and of even temper had been known to show a ruthless and unforgiving streak if crossed or betrayed. He was now an old man but in age only as his men knew of his unremitting appetite for conquest and attainment of wealth.

When the small fleet left the harbour the weather was warm with a small westerly to ease them along the north coast of Cornwall and then east along the English Channel. The Tempest and Storm led the way followed by the three Polaccas intent on intercepting the English somewhere down the east coast of England. The plans were set, the weather fine and Jan felt uplifted by the thought of the capture of an English treasure.

*   *   *

I hung on to the rigging as the brig I was travelling on tacked out of the harbour and set sail to travel south along the East Coast of England. It was a bright day accompanied by a pleasant and helpful wind, which filled the sheets of my transport and those of the schooner that was now skimming past throwing up a sparkling bow wave and a fair amount of spray. It was a fine sight and I returned the wave of Captain Lopez who was aboard the schooner. I had not known the whole plan until very recently and now seeing the relative speed of the two vessels, both under full canvass; the preparations seemed to make sense.

The brig was relatively large and very well armed and initially seemed to me to be exactly what was needed to protect the boxes of treasure. I had seen large boxes being brought onto the brig with a well-armed escort and I and the rest of Duncan's troop had also been alert and well armed during the transportation. Captain Lopez however had boarded the schooner, which when it had taken on its supplies with a lot less fuss, had quickly moved out into deep water. Why Captain Lopez was not on our vessel was only explained to us by Duncan after we had sailed, when he also outlined the main aspects of the plan he and the Captain had in mind if we came across any problems while sailing to our destination in The Netherlands.

The East coast of England was not one I was familiar with and for much of the day the mixture of cliffs, estuaries and long sandy beaches made fascinating viewing. Luke and I spent some of the time discussing the news we had heard about the wins and losses of the recent campaigns and it seemed that there was no clear winner of the conflict at this point. Small battles seemed to be mostly won by the Royalists but it also seemed that more and more areas of the country were becoming hostile towards the King. Luke and I agreed that the outcome could easily be swung by outside assistance along the lines of which could be precipitated by our present escapade.

Luke pointed to the schooner, which was now well ahead of us but still clearly in sight.

'Let's hope he doesn't come rushing back to us with news as it can only be bad.'

He also pointed to some dolphins, which were now leaping out alongside us and we both watched them in silence until a call from Duncan jolted us back to reality.

'We will meet in the Captain's cabin lads, go and fetch the others.'

Luke and I found Sam and Joe below decks checking their weapons and we all trooped off to the meeting.

Duncan went over the plan in more detail and pointed out that everyone should be sure we knew the possible consequences of the plan.

'It is quite likely that news of the treasure has been spread to those who might want to relieve us of it and we must be prepared to fight this vessel for as long as possible if we contact an enemy. You have all been assigned to various parts of the ship and the captain assures me his men will give no quarter to attackers. He also thinks that we are in most danger as we near the English Channel where an inhospitable coastline and a narrowing channel would be an ideal area for an attack.

The schooner is now well ahead of us and will turn towards us at any sign of trouble.'

* * *

Jan's fleet sailed unmolested along the English Channel with the Storm in the lead and the rest following in line. On reaching the southern part of the North Sea it was time to put plans into action.

'Signal the fleet to take up patrol positions,' ordered Jan.

Gradually the pattern of the patrol order could be seen as the fleet started to string out in a line east to west with Jan's vessel and the other Xebec in the centre and two of the Polaccas moving out to the east and the other keeping relatively close to the shore. The distance between the various vessels increased as they spread their net, hoping to snare their prey. It took three hours for the fleet to sail into position and from any one ship another was just in sight so that flag messages could be sent and received. Jan stood on the quarterdeck of The Storm but said little until he noticed a sailor carelessly bash his pipe on the side of the craft. Jan bellowed at the sailor who was dragged by the quartermaster up the steps to the position where Jan was surveying the scene.

'You fool, can't you see the powder being brought to the guns; do you want to blow us all up?'

Before he could answer the sailor felt the full force of Jan's fist in his face, which broke the man's nose in a splattering of blood.

'Take him below, half rations for two days and during that time perhaps you will think about your actions, idiot.'

The brutal side of Jan accompanied the educated side, which cared for his crew. This harsh side showed no quarter to those who betrayed him or failed to follow his orders and he had committed many barbarous acts when he felt they could be of benefit. The burning of a church in Ireland containing English inhabitants too old for slavery was done to impress the Irish, a strategy that seemed to have worked according to members of the crew.

Again alone on the windward aft section of the quarterdeck Jan turned his head to look towards the European mainland and thoughts turned to his daughter now back in The Netherlands. He missed her gentle company and he stared over the taffrail down at the wake flowing from the stern and rudder below for some moments before his thoughts returned to the task at hand. He looked to the west where the Polacca could clearly be seen outlined along the coast and then to the east where the other Xebec had taken up its station. Neither was showing signal flags and as evening was approaching Jan hoped the English would not evade them in the dark. Keeping station at night was difficult and all the fleet had lights blazing to keep them on station and again Jan wondered if the English might spot the beacons and silently slip through his net. Leaving Asif in charge Jan eventually went down to his cabin leaving instructions that he was to be woken at the sight of any vessel. No news came and he rose before dawn hoping for an early sighting of the enemy. The first sighting however did not come until late in the afternoon when lookouts shouted that the Xebec to the east was signalling that a sail had been spotted dead ahead. All eyes and Jan's long glass was now straining to find the target, which was soon spotted by men who were lookouts high on the mainmast.

Jan ordered an increase in sail and flag messages were hoisted to the western Polacca which started to speed towards the target. Jan could see no reason why the ships to the east would not now be homing in on the sail in the distance, which according to shouts from atop the unidentified mast had turned one hundred and eighty degrees and was hightailing it back to the north.

*   *   *

Luke and I were in the middle of a practice session with one of the gun crews when a shout from above revealed that the schooner was returning at some speed. Alongside the other men we completed the gun routine before returning to the deck where it was now clear the schooner was being chased by at least three ships and soon afterwards captain Brown ordered that the ship should clear for action.

The routine had been practiced many times and Luke and I took up our positions alongside some musketeers on deck. There was always some excitement during the practices with crews competing for the best times; however it was obvious this was no drill and a serious atmosphere immediately enveloped the proceedings. Sam and Joe were nearby and Joe winked at me as our eyes met. Silence was demanded in these circumstances so that orders could be heard above the noise of preparing the guns and men running to their positions.

Within an hour the schooner was close to our brig and it could be seen that five vessels were homing in on their prey in a pincer movement. There were two large, heavily sailed ships now directly ahead, one smaller vessel cutting in from the west and two more curving around from the open sea to the east. The schooner sailed rapidly past us and as per plan we sailed straight into the jaws of the trap. As fast as the schooner disappeared out of view to the north the enemy started closing in on us seemingly ignoring the fleeing escort.

I heard Captain Brown instruct Mr Phillips the sailing master to be prepared to sail between the two ships to the west.

'They will probably expect us to head for open sea especially with this westerly but I want us close hauled between those two on my mark.'

The sailing master was obviously clear about the instructions and issued orders to the men below the quarterdeck.

The larger of the two landward vessels was now only one hundred yards away steering head on, straight for us.

'Two points to starboard Mr Phillips if you please and Lieutenant instruct the port battery to fire as they bear.'

With a series of great crashes the port cannon blasted away as the large boat came alongside and before the smoke settled the enemy responded with a broadside of their own.

I felt the rush of air as a cannon ball passed over my head to land harmlessly in the sea beyond but other shot made their mark. The enemy was aiming at the rigging and a crash of timber brought ropes and spars down onto the deck.

The smaller boat on the starboard side started firing but received a devastating broadside from our brig's starboard battery. The noise of cannon and crashing timber didn't however drown out the shouts and screams of injured men and after untangling myself from fallen rigging I started firing at the large vessel which was now almost past us and seemed to be turning around the stern.

'Hard to starboard,' ordered Captain Brown.

The two ships were now in a tight dance around each other, the enemy trying to rake the brig from the stern and the brig turning to meet out another broadside. During the turn the brig was hit in the stern by a few shots but quickly came around to send another broadside into the large enemy, which seemed to stagger under the weight of shot.

As I looked around I could see Luke, Sam, Duncan and Joe as they all rushed to the starboard side to fire their muskets at targets on the enemy's deck but as they did so a sudden crash seemed to shudder through the whole ship and men including myself went skidding and flying across the deck. The smaller enemy had rammed the brig.

'Repel boarders,' ordered the captain.

The smaller ship's crew were now beginning to jump onto our foredeck but were met by a screaming group of our seamen.

'Musketeers to the quarterdeck,' shouted Captain Brown.

We scuttled up the ladder and all five of us sent a volley of shot into the pirates standing on the edge of their boat. This seemed to stem the tide of men and with a mighty crash one of our starboard cannon hammered grape across the main deck sweeping men away as though a mighty hand had just brushed them aside.

Our brig was still stuck fast by the bow when the devastating and final blow of the battle happened. Just as we seemed to be getting the upper hand the small boat shot, what sounded like two cannon, through one of our gunports. This must have ignited gunpowder as the front of our brig exploded in a sheet of flames. We were all thrown backwards like rag dolls crashing against the rear rails of the quarterdeck.

The next thing I remember was being dragged out of freezing cold water by my hair, I lashed out but felt weak and powerless as strong hands held me down in the bottom of a small and violently rocking boat. I retched into the bottom of the boat as I coughed up seawater and I felt my arms being tied behind my back.

'Sit him over here,' said a strongly accented voice.

I was unceremoniously dumped on my backside in the stern of the boat next to a large, heavily moustached man who had the largest sword I have ever seen resting by his side.

'How many survivors Asif?' shouted a voice from above.

'Probably about a dozen, that blast killed nearly everyone not in the aft section of the brig,' he replied.

I was shoved through a gun port of the large vessel that loomed over us and then dragged onto the deck where I was pushed onto the planks alongside other prisoners. I was hardly conscious but I felt a strong urge to see if my friends were there, which to my delight they were. Bedraggled and with cuts and bruises the other four sat tied up along the side of the boat. Nobody spoke but I felt suddenly far more alive than I probably looked on seeing that they had all survived.

There was much chatter around us in what seemed like many different languages until suddenly a large man cut a swathe through the pirates and there was an immediate silence.

'Where is the treasure you English cur?' he bellowed aiming a kick at the sailor nearest to him.

'Let me ask them,' said the huge man with the massive sword.

On unsheathing his sword the sailor nearest to him bleated, 'on the schooner, the treasure is on the schooner.'

The two pirates looked at each other before turning to look in the direction of the schooner, which presumably was now well out of sight.

'We will never catch the bastard now,' fumed the pirate leader. 'Lock this lot up, at least we can collect some slave money.'

We were taken below and squeezed into the foremost section of the forecastle, which was dark, wet and cramped. A door was locked behind us and we were trapped in a hellhole.

'Luke, Duncan, Sam, Joe, are you alright?' I asked into the blackness.

Each man in turn answered that they were not badly injured and the other five surviving sailors told us their names, some of which I knew although I could see none of them.

'So the plan worked then,' said Joe, 'with us being the bait in the trap.'

'That's just about it,' replied Duncan, 'except we were really just expected to delay the pirates for as long as possible probably eventually overwhelming them. No one knew they would come in such force and the explosion was just bad luck.'

What happened to our brig?' I asked.

'She went down and pulled the Polacca down with her, we are the only ones who made it,' said Joe. 'We were all blown off the stern and luckily we were able to hang on to some planking. Duncan dragged you onto our raft until we were 'rescued' by this lot.'

For the next two days we were left in our cell except for two visits to the deck where we were treated roughly but allowed to crap over the side of the boat and also have a meal. We were warned not to soil our cell or we would all be whipped and we were spat on and kicked by passing pirates who laughed at our predicament.

On the second day we entered the Bristol Channel, according to Sam, and were approaching the Isle of Lundy when our visit to the deck was cut short. A shout from the masthead seemed to create concern among our captors and we were quickly bundled back into our cell.

'I had heard there were pirates on Lundy and it seems that all is not well,' said Sam.

The noise on deck indicated the pirates were readying themselves for action, which started with a series of cannon shots in the distance. Eventually our pirate boat also fired and was definitely hit in return.

'It looks as though someone has decided to get rid of the Mosselmen,' said Joe in the blackness.

From the shouts and crashing of timber it seemed our pirate was being severely hit and it was not long before a sudden change of direction indicated a possible retreat.

We were to learn later that the merchants of Bristol had organised a raid on the island, had released over five hundred prisoners and sunk one pirate boat in the harbour along with the two Polaccas that were in the fleet that had attacked us. Our Xebec called 'The Storm' was also quite badly mauled and along with the other Xebec, 'The Tempest' had made a run for it towards the south.

It was not until the day after the battle that we were allowed back on deck where the damage to the boat and the crew became more obvious. There were normally three lanteen sails on our boat but the central mast was down and the crew were working hard to repair other damage. While on deck the pirates seemed to ignore us for longer than usual and Sam pointed out that the other Xebec seemed undamaged and was escorting us to windward.

'I have seen these boats before,' said Sam, 'they are fast but are not really designed for high seas and it looks as though we are in for a bit of a blow.' We all turned to look in the westerly direction of his gaze and could clearly see the darkening sky despite the fact it was nearly midday.

The storm only lasted a few hours but our boat was thrown around and it felt as if we were taking on water. This soon became completely evident when we were roughly pulled out of our cell and put to work on the hand pumps. We worked as hard as we could and although a couple of well armed pirates slapped a few of us occasionally it was quite obvious we were pumping to save our own lives as well as theirs and therefore did not need much encouragement. When the storm abated we were allowed to slow down and take the pumping process in turns until completely exhausted we were relieved by other sailors who looked more like slaves than pirates. The next three days were a mixture of pumping or sitting on deck and we were only sent to our cell at night.

We were sailing south and the weather was warm and pleasant on deck and we even seemed to be fed rather better than before although we were still treated with open contempt by our Islamic captors. Looking across at the other Xebec Duncan pointed out that they also seemed to have suffered in the storm as their front mast was tilting at a strange angle. We had now settled into a routine which although arduous did not seem life threatening. When I mentioned this to Duncan he pointed out that we were prime slave commodities and that we would be worth more if undamaged. This brought us all into a state of near despair and some of the other sailors with us broke down at the outward stating of this fact which we had all tried to ignore. Duncan although bluff in nature was also a natural leader and he assured them that he for one would be no slave and that if they followed his lead we may all still have a chance of escaping. This chance arose rather more quickly than expected and not in the way any of us could have envisaged.

We were off the coast of Portugal, according to one of the pirates who could speak English, when a shout from a lookout had all the pirates looking towards the coast. A stream of small fast boats was heading for the Tempest, which was like us struggling for speed. Both of the Xebecs were well armed but our boat was certainly low on manpower and I estimated there were only seventy to eighty men aboard. If the Tempest were similarly poorly crewed, like us it would find it difficult to service all its guns and repel a determined raid. The Tempest was attacked first and although it was not boarded it was soon being assaulted on all sides by at least eight boats all flying red flags.

'Red flags, that means no prisoners,' said Sam,' it seems as though this lot are out for revenge.'

The situation was now critical with the shortage of men and the number of enemy boats being against us. It was at this point that our situation changed dramatically. The pirate Captain strode over to us with his massive guard.

'Gentlemen, we have a predicament,' he said in a strong Dutch accent.

'I am Captain Jan Janszoon, you may have heard of me. I captured you and intended to place you on the Moroccan slave market in Sale. This I may still do, however you have a chance to change this possibility. As you can see we are under attack, seemingly from an old enemy of mine who is out for blood. The red flags mean he will kill everyone he captures and be assured he will carry out his threat. I now have only a skeleton crew after our various skirmishes and I am offering you a truce. If you fight for me to help save us I will free you all if we escape. On this you have the word of Murat Rais, which, as all that know me would testify, has always been true.' With this his guard bowed his head in acknowledgement.

I spoke out first by saying that we were ready to defend ourselves even if it meant fighting alongside our captors before realising I was speaking for everyone but they all readily agreed. We were quickly released and given muskets. The five seamen with us were given a gun to man and we took up our places to help repel an attack.

The other Xebec was struggling to fend off the advances of the many small fast craft, which were seemingly brimming with enemy corsairs. Their canon fire seemed ineffective and inaccurate and the small boats were preparing to board. The enemy probably expected us to try to escape in our damaged craft and seemed to be ignoring us. Seeing this Murat Rais gave the order to beat towards the other Xebec. Despite lacking a major sail we sped towards the small boats and managed a broadside, which caused carnage on one craft and damaged another. We were within musket distance and a volley from all those manning the side caused more enemy casualties. Despite our efforts the enemy continued with their attack but now their strength had been split between two large if poorly manned craft. Our gunner showed his skills by sinking another marauder before a number of their craft came alongside and sent men swarming up grappling ropes onto our deck. Hand to hand fighting broke out all along our starboard side and a large hairy corsair came at me with a sword. Luckily I had reloaded and shot him at point blank range in the chest and he flew backwards

over the side taking another pirate with him.
I dropped my musket and picked up the
sword he had dropped and charged at two
men who had cornered Duncan. I slashed
one man across his unprotected neck and
Duncan smashed the other in the face with
his musket. I could see Luke, Sam and Joe
fighting with swords and was about to go
to their aid when our gun crew came up
from the hold screaming. They charged into
the pirates who for a moment were taken
aback by the attack. I looked around to see
Murat Rais' bodyguard fighting ferociously
below the quarterdeck but I could also see
our corsair Captain was being surrounded
by a group of baying pirates. I shouted to
Duncan who followed me up the steps to the
quarterdeck where we laid into the pirates
and chopped them down before they could
kill the one man who could possibly save us.
Down below on the main deck the crew had
got the better of our attackers who were now
streaming back down ropes or jumping over
the side. I shouted to the gun crew to go back
and try and sink more vessels, which they did
with consummate skill. The other Xebec had
also managed to fend off the foe and both
boats were now putting on sail to move away
from the small flotilla, which seemed to have

lost heart and was retreating to the safety of the coast.

There were many men dead or injured on the deck including two of our gun crew who, though alive, were both in a bad way. Although they had been our captors having fought alongside the crew it seemed only natural to try and help them with their injuries. Luke and I splinted a man's leg using some thin planking and I could see Duncan and the others giving similar assistance elsewhere. Soon afterwards we were assigned tasks around the boat, which was barely seaworthy but obviously valuable to its owner who was either shouting orders vigorously or providing sympathy and kind words to his injured crew members.

There was a pause in our activity when a basic meal was provided at which point the captain approached our group as we squatted alongside the broken mainmast. At his approach we all stood up, I am not sure whether out of respect or fear but it seemed to be the natural thing for a sailor to do when confronted by a captain.

'You fought well and I am forever in your debt for saving my life and helping to save our boat. When we return to Morocco you are free men and will be my guests until transport can be found for your return. You will be safe in my home despite being infidels, which might be a problem to you if you move away from my protection. Again I thank you but would now ask you to continue to work as crewmembers until our safe arrival in Safi.'

After another two days we were obviously sailing close to the north west coast of Africa as the mountains in the distance could be seen as well as desert sand reaching down to the sea. During this time we were allowed to move freely in the vessel and the crew seemed to treat us nearly as equals although being Christian and not Muslim did create a barrier. As a group we spent time talking about what the future might hold but as this was so uncertain, it was difficult to make any judgements or decisions. A few of the gun crew however seemed quite impressed by the lifestyle of a corsair, which according to the crew provided wealth and adventure while not being oppressed. They were free to sail under any commander and they felt their captain was both fair and successful. Some of the corsairs were English though most were North African or Southern European. The one thing they had in common was they had all converted to Islam, which was compulsory in order that they could join the corsairs of the Barbary Coast.

We sailed into Safi where canon fire from an overlooking castle greeted our arrival. The harbour was teeming with small craft and there were two large Xebecs anchored at the southern end under the castle walls.

Our boat anchored alongside the other large vessels and our captain called a muster of all the crew onto the deck. He and Asif made a stirring sight in their refinery and he addressed us all in English then Spanish and Arabic.

'Men you have served me bravely and will be rewarded for your efforts and loyalty. The treasures and slaves we have gained will provide you all with wealth enough to retire to your tents in the Desert.'

This bought a cheer and a laugh from the men standing on the deck.

'The monies owed to you will be paid out in the usual manner after the slaves have been sold and the treasure valued by our Jewish treasurers.'

This was followed by a playful booing and again laughter all-round.

'There are some amongst you who were taken for slaves but risked your lives to help us survive and are henceforth set free and will therefore will not gain us value at the markets.'

This was followed by us being slapped heartily on the back by some of the surrounding corsairs who again booed cheerfully at our lack of value.

'I will leave my officers to attend to the ship's needs and the rest of you are free to leave my charge as soon as the bum boats arrive. However I will say that if any of you wish to sail with me again you are welcome under my flag.'

A final big cheer went up from the men who then started to drift away to collect their belongings in readiness to leave the boat. For a few moments we eight, because two of the gun crew had died of their injuries, stood around rather at a loss until the huge Asif invited us into the captain's quarters.

'You have served me well and I thank you. This will tide you over and help to pay for a passage home,' he said as Asif gave each of us a pouch of coins.

'You will be safe in Safi although you must also be wary of those who might try to take advantage. I will provide you with accommodation amongst my servants' quarters but you are free to come and go as you please. I ask you to keep Musabi informed as

to your activities and to tell him if you have
issues. He will also try to gain passage for
you all back to England. Thank you again
gentlemen, we may meet again but until then
I have appointed Musabi as your escort.' With
that we were dismissed and within an hour
we were being escorted onto a small awaiting
boat by Musabi, one of the captain's officers,
who explained that he would be willing to
show us around the city once we had settled
into our accommodation.

Viewed from the small boat the city of
Safi stretched around the bay in front of
us with the large sandstone castle reaching
out into the sea to the south and the desert
surrounding the sun-baked buildings. None
of us had ever seen such a sight and the heat
of the day, despite being late in the year, was
fierce and unrelenting as it reflected off the
clear, blue and calm water of the bay.

On landing we walked through the Souk
and past a great mosque before reaching
the castle. Built of sandstone it reflected
like red fire in the late afternoon sun and
we entered through a main gate in the high
walls. Armed guards on the gate greeted
Musabi with respect and we passed into
the inner courtyard where the shade and a
central walled pool, with many green plants

surrounding it, created a cool and pleasant atmosphere. This corsair obviously lived well in the splendour of the castle surrounded by his loyal followers who, although not ostentatiously rich, were certainly well off by the look of their clothes.

Our quarters, a barrack room, which probably housed soldiers in the past, were basic but clean and servants soon brought us food and water. We gathered together to talk over our situation which had turned out better than we could possibly have thought a couple of days earlier but also posed a number of questions.

There were eight of us, including the remaining members of the gun crew, and although Duncan was our natural leader in conflict I felt a responsibility to all of them as I had led them into this situation.

'I will talk to Musabi about getting a boat back to England as soon as possible but I doubt if that is likely to happen immediately. Until then we should make sure we do not antagonise our hosts but at the same time it should be interesting to find out more about this piratical band and the culture of the local people.'

Over the next three weeks it became obvious that we could be in Morocco for some time as the corsairs were plundering most of the boats they came across that might have given us passage and according to Musabi, Murat Rais was anxious that a reliable and safe passage be found for us. During this time we had all been enthralled by the local culture and the three members of the gun crew had become so impressed by the free lifestyle of the corsairs, compared to the strict and overbearing English society that they had decided to join their new found friends.

'These men sail the seas as free men, gather riches beyond our wildest dreams and live to a code we can easily understand. We hope you do not object to our decision as we will be leaving today,' said Jed, one of the gun crew.

'You are free to make up your own minds,' I said 'but surely you must have family at home and by the way would you not have to convert to the Islamic faith if you stay?' I pointed out.

'None of us are married and maybe someday we will return, but as far as faith is concerned we have agreed that if that is what is required we will do it, after all both religions agree there is just one god, the rules in order to follow a religion have basically been created by men. We feel men in different parts of the world have just created their own set of ways of worshiping.'

With that they left and we never saw them again although we had heard that Jed had become quite a success due to his knowledge of ships guns.

Chapter Nine

THE HUNT

Each day we had a basic ritual of washing, being fed by the servants, wandering the streets of the Souk and investigating the coming and going of the various shipping until after a month of frustrating lack of action or progress, we were summoned to one of the offices in the castle where we were greeted by an obviously flamboyant Italian.

'I am Captain Allesandri and although we have not met I saw your deeds from the quarterdeck of the Xebec that accompanied you. My Polacca was sunk but myself and many of my crew were rescued by the Xebec and we were all impressed by the way you fought to save our leader Murat Rais. Now I realise you were also probably trying to save yourselves but nevertheless you have become respected men amongst the corsairs and I am pleased to make your acquaintance.

The reason I have asked you here is to say that unfortunately we have still not managed to find suitable passage for you and as the northern winter is now approaching, the stormy weather may mean you will have to stay for some time.'

It was the end of September when we left, it was now the second week of November and although we all realised it might take some time for us to gain a return passage this news was deflating.

'To relieve some of your disappointment I would like to take you on a hunting trip into the mountains and the desert where you will see animals and sights you can see nowhere else. I see only three of you are here today but the invitation is for all five of you if you so wish. We leave at dawn tomorrow and Musabi will explain what you need. I look forward to seeing you tomorrow and thank you again for your heroic deeds.'

These corsairs put great store in loyalty and helping each other and we seemed to have been accepted amongst them in a way we had previously felt would be impossible.

Sam and Joe, who had not been at our meeting with Captain Allesandri, decided not to go on the trip as they had befriended some fishermen.

'We have been invited to go fishing along the coast and we think we will be more at home on the water than on the back of a camel although some say there is not much difference. We also felt we could keep an eye on the traffic to see if a possible return passage can be found,' said Joe.

The next day Sam and Joe left to meet the fishermen as we were escorted to the camels and horses which had gathered on the dusty ground outside the castle walls. We had been given garments similar to the other men who were mingling around the animals.

'I see you are dressed for the occasion,' said the approaching Allesandri, 'you will find the garb most appropriate for where we are going.'

We had each been given a brown, long, loose fitting outer garment that had large sleeves and a hood that came to a point. Although very different to our own clothes it was easy to see how the djellaba, as it was called, would protect us from the sun and blown sand.

'The colour denotes you are all bachelors, so I hope this is appropriate as the local women are likely to react accordingly,' said a laughing Allesandri, who was a character we would all soon come to like and admire.

There were about forty animals and thirty men on the expedition. The men were all well armed with long muskets and swords and Duncan said he felt rather naked without a weapon of some sort. Allesandri heard his comment and rapped a few short orders in Arabic to some men who came over to us. They invited us into a nearby large mud built building, which was crammed full of weapons of every possible type.

'Please take whichever you wish,' said one of the men who then pointed out some of the best weapons. We all selected an appropriate sword, (although I felt Luke's scimitar was rather overdoing the absorbing of local culture) and a musket with ammunition. I also noticed a large and interestingly shaped bow on the wall. I pointed to this and the men climbed up to retrieve it looking at me rather sceptically. I checked the bow and the strings which were kept in a small leather pouch and I was amazed at the workmanship and potential power of the bow. I had heard of these small curved bows but never actually seen one. It was light and made of two different woods with the two limbs bending away from the belly of the bow. The arrows were in two large grass baskets and I sorted out the best fifty which the men put into a leather bag and gave me a leather holder that held a dozen arrows and could be attached to a belt. Having claimed our weapons we were given a quick lesson in how to mount a camel, which turned out to be just as difficult as it looks. After a few circles of the parade ground, led by the helper and trying out his instructions on how to control the beast, we set off in a line towards the mountains to the east.

During the middle of the day we stopped at a small village where we were fed by local people who tended to our animals and were obviously in awe of Captain Allesandri.

'I notice your influence is not just along the coast Captain,' I said.

'Your observation is correct Solomon; we have brought wealth and protection to the people of Safi and the surrounding districts. There are many tribal people to the East and South who covert our wealth so it is in our interest to keep the local people on our side. Only a few months ago some nomads raided this place but luckily we had a patrol nearby and they chased the raiders off before too much damage was done. We are well armed just in case we come across such a group again although my information is that there are no insurgents for one hundred miles. I have been hunting here for five years and never encountered any such problems so let us enjoy the thrill of the hunt.'

We continued our travels until it was dark when the men set up tents on a bank overlooking a dry wadi. There was a hierarchy amongst the men and it seemed only us three and Musabi was expected to eat with and converse with the captain.

'These men are not corsairs but local tribesmen who work for us,' explained Musabi as he showed us where to sit on the blankets arranged around a fire. We ate a stew of meat and vegetables and drank goats' milk freshly gained from one of the villages we passed and our conversations led to how our Italian captain became a corsair. He said he hoped like us, to one day return to Europe but not until he had made the fortune he would need to live in the style for which he had always wished. Yes, he had been a Christian Knight and was now a converted Islamic pirate captain but although he was also an ambitious man these ambitions related to his home in Venice, as he was loyal to Murat Rais who was his greatest friend despite once being captured by him just as we had been captured.

'We have that fact in common,' said Allesandri, 'along with the fact that we helped him and he returns the favour with his loyalty to us, he is indeed a great man although I must point out that he is not a man to be crossed.'

With that in mind Allesandri related some of the tales of Murat Rais which both shocked and amazed us. He was indeed a man you would rather have on your side. We had both fought him and fought alongside him and I hoped we would not have to make a choice about him in the future.

Camel riding was uncomfortable to say the least at first, but the swaying motion was so like that of a boat on a rolling swell that we all soon adapted to the movement although getting the animals to take notice of instructions was another skill altogether. On the second day of our travels we started to climb up a wide valley where villagers grew crops along the side of a streambed. The valley bottom was perhaps a mile wide but by nightfall the width had decreased to a tenth of that size and the steepness of the slope increased significantly. That night our colleagues started to explain what we were hunting. We had naturally thought perhaps we would be after deer and in fact that was the first thing we did kill for food the next day, but to our surprise and also shock it seemed we were after lion as Musabi explained.

'The villagers along the valley have lost some animals and one child to a lion a few days ago. We mean to track and kill the lion, which if we are successful will be of great significance to our standing with the locals.

Some of their men have tracked the lion so far but do not wish to venture too far from home when Berber bandits might be in the vicinity.'

It took us the whole of the next day to reach a pass in the hills where we camped and were told the trackers would meet us the next morning and as the lion seemed to moving away from us towards the desert we would have to act fast before it disappeared into the wilderness.

After setting up camp and eating a fine meal of goat meat and fruit I decided to try out my recurved bow. I unstrapped the arrows and walked away from the camp towards a thicket of trees, which would be my target. A few of the tribesmen could see what I was doing and followed me laughing and joking with each other and seemingly looking back to the camp expecting something. I strung my bow and examined the arrows before nocking one and letting fly at a tree some fifty yards away. The arrow hit the trunk but at a slightly lower height than I expected. A few more arrows made me realise the bow was light but powerful and I was impressed by its potential. The arrows were iron tipped and lovingly made; this had surely been the warbow of an important person. Suddenly from behind a dune came a man on horseback riding straight for us with a bow in hand. He raised the bow and shot an arrow at the same tree that was my target which he hit dead centre. This was horsemanship and bowmanship of the highest calibre and was obviously much enjoyed by the dozen tribesmen who fell about cheering and laughing. My effort did not match the horseman's skill but I meant to change that. This time I aimed at a tree over one hundred yards away and shot four arrows into the trunk in quick succession, which brought rapturous applause from the watching throng and even the horseman applauded with a big smile on his face. He trotted over, dismounted and asked if I could shoot from the horse. I am an excellent horseman and have shot a bow from horseback before and this bow was designed to be used from the saddle. Rather showing off I leapt onto the horse with my bow across my back and charged the onlookers who scattered as I pulled the horse to a sudden halt in front of them. I then spun the horse round and galloped past the trees into which I fired three arrows which all struck a different tree smack in the middle. The men fell about laughing and cheering again and when I dismounted, they all surrounded me with slaps on the back and huge smiles on their faces. After retrieving the arrows we all returned to the camp and the men were chattering excitedly as we were met by captain Allesandri who called us over.

'We have heard from the trackers who inform us that the lion has gone into the desert. We will eat and have two hours rest and then move on.'

This we did although travelling at night was difficult, luckily the full moon provided us with enough light on this cloudless, starlit night for us to be able to travel at a good pace. We stopped to rest again and we all slept until dawn after which we quickly ate and broke camp before setting off, accompanied by the trackers, over the pass and down into the desert.

To the east the dunes seemed never ending and to the south the desert was rock strewn and almost impassable. Even I could see the tracks and Luke was soon amongst the leading tribesmen developing his already considerable tracking skills. Duncan had spent much of his time talking to the Captain and they trotted together at the head of the column while I intermingled with our escort. It seemed that the lion was also following prey as sable hoof prints had been identified alongside that of the lion. The men thought this might help us as if the lion made a kill it would probably rest alongside its meal. It was therefore a complete shock when two lions suddenly appeared running full tilt at Allesandri and Duncan at the head of our column. Without thinking or panicking I snatched an arrow from my holder and fired at the lead lion. I hit him square in the shoulder and he fell sideways into the path of the second lion whose charge was suddenly halted. I fired two arrows at the second lion just as a number of muskets finished off the two beasts.

In the quiet of the aftermath some of the tribesmen moved carefully around the area checking to see if any more cats were to be seen but there were none. Luke had been one of those who had shot the lion and our whole group now collected around the dead animals, first in awe and then in relief that the job had been done without casualties. The size of the animals especially their heads astonished me and Luke and I stood for some minutes before we dare touch the fine beasts and the tribesmen then moved in and started to strip the skins which were then set out on litters and dragged behind two of the horses.

Captain Allesandri had planned to return to Safi via the port of Sale, which he said had been the base for the corsairs or 'Sale Rovers' as they had been called, for many years. He wished to visit the slave auction (the one we could have finished up in) adding that it would be the best place to sell the lion skins. I felt uncomfortable with the thought of the slave auction, but Duncan and Luke agreed we should not upset our hosts by complaining as we could have so easily have been up for sale ourselves.

Chapter Ten

THE BERBER RAID

O ur expected return journey to Safi was to be interrupted following the news related to the Captain by some of his scouts.

'It seems a group of Berbers are in the vicinity after all,' Allesandri informed us.

'They recently attacked a village not far from here and captured a number of women, presumably for slaves. I must try and find these tribesmen and attempt to retrieve the women if we are to continue to enjoy the favour of the villagers.'

Allesandri gave us the opportunity to return to Safi with an escort but the three of us decided to help the Captain in his quest.

'My men have already gained fresh camels and provisions and we leave within the hour. The Berbers travel fast and can be very illusive; they know the desert and will have some advantages over us. We however, have a strong force of over thirty; including yourselves and my own Berber scouts will be a great asset.'

I had seen and met a number of Berbers during my time in Morocco and they were looked upon as a lesser tribe although they were renowned for their desert survival and fighting skills. They dressed differently to our Arab and corsair hosts and often wore brightly coloured clothes and exotically painted their faces. This was obviously going to be a difficult mission but I could see that Duncan and Luke were becoming quite animated in their excitement of trying to track the Berbers in the desert.

After four hours of camel travel, which I still found to be quite nauseating, we arrived at the village where the raid had taken place. We were met by what turned out to be the headman of the settlement who proceeded to provide information about the attackers; usefully I could now understand much of what he related as my Arabic was something I had tried to develop in the past months.

It transpired that about ten Berbers had attacked at dawn and having killed four of the local men who tried to resist them had left taking three young women with them. The headman seemed to stress not only his sadness but also a certain amount of surprise in that until now the village had been on good terms with local Bedouins and had traded with them frequently stressing that they were mostly quiet farming people.

'I don't think we are looking for local Bedouins but more likely it is a raiding band from the interior nomads,' stated Allesandri.

We followed our scouts who were tracking the trail left by the raiders. The tracks were relatively easy to follow although how Luke could surmise the number of riders was beyond me. It was agreed that we were following a group of sixteen horses which again pointed to bandits being the tough nomads of the desert. It seemed they also had four camels which were heavily laden probably with grain and water for the horses. As we moved into the desert the sand seemed to radiate the heat so that conditions were furnace like and almost painful despite our appropriate clothing. We were determined to lose as little time as possible and the trek continued during the hottest part of day, with even the tough Duncan shaking his head in disbelief when I grimaced in his direction.

The camp we set up when night fell was a quiet reserved affair due to the exertions of the day and the seriousness of the situation which was emphasized by the fact, that one of the women taken was a close relative of one of our trackers. We all took turns to be on guard duty and a fire was made out of the dry thorn bushes which surrounded the camp and this helped restore moral whilst also providing a very welcome hot meal. There were a few jokes thrown around about not needing a fire to frighten off the lions, with us having the 'Lion Man,' in our midst but the frivolity soon turned to quiet reflection.

It was a fitful sleep from which I awoke the next morning as the night had been cold and the sound of yapping jackals had somewhat unnerved me. After a hasty and meagre breakfast we continued our pursuit until we came across a small uninhabited waterhole surrounded by a few dozen palm trees. After some casting around the scouts returned to say the band we were following had evenly split into two with one group setting off in an easterly direction and the other more to the south.

'We have enough provisions for about four days,' started Allesandri after he had called us all together.

I will take half of us after the group travelling south east and Musabi will lead the rest to the east. We will all meet back here

in two days time. Whoever returns here first
will wait for one day and a night and then
return to Safi and report to Murat Rais and he
will know what to do.

Duncan, Luke and I were included in
Allesandri's party and we had no problem
following the tracks left by our quarry and
the scouts felt we were gaining on them,
however the whole expedition was thrown
into chaos during the late afternoon. I had
noticed the sky in the distance seemed to be
getting very hazy with a sort of purple tinge
and the wind which previously had been
light suddenly increased.

'Sandstorm,' was the sudden warning
and the men in front started to down their
camels and were in the process of climbing
off as two things hit us at the same time. The
sand blew straight at us from the east in a
blinding and stinging rage which caught me
off guard as did the sight of a blurred line of
sword wielding horsemen charging into our
midst. I saw a number of our men go down
in front of me although I knew Luke and
Duncan were behind me and therefore safe
for the moment.

The crack of a rifle from behind felled
a horseman charging straight at me and the
sight of the tumbling horse and rider spooked

my camel which loped off at surprising speed into the raging sand cloud. How long we galloped away for I was not sure and although I continually tried to calm the beast it eventually stopped of its own accord. I hauled my mount down, covered its face with my blanket and huddled down in the lee of its large body. Throughout the ordeal of stinging sand and noisy wind the animal sat quietly although it did seem we might soon turn into a dune by the amount of sand accumulating around us.

As quickly as the storm had arrived it relented almost as suddenly, although visibility was now limited as night was drawing in. The camel seemed reluctant to stand at first but eventually I was on board and searching the horizon for any signs of life; I saw none.

During our tracking I had been using the compass given to me by Betsy and although I had no idea where I was at least I felt I could retrace a route back to the coast if I could not contact the rest of the party.

The storm had completely obliterated all tracks and the dunes were no help in providing any landmarks. I was wondering how local tribesmen seemed to know their way without any form of navigation when I noticed two horsemen watching me from the crest of a dune to the east. I stood for a moment staring at the riders before retreating behind my standing camel. The men did not seem to be armed with guns but I quickly unhitched my bow from my pack on the back of the camel. They started to trot and slide down the side of the dune with expert control and I could see their swords hanging menacingly by their sides. They stopped about fifty yards away and one waved in a seemingly friendly way. I lowered my bow and they slowly advanced.

'Effendi; Killer of the Lion', shouted one of the men, 'we are here to help you'.

The men explained they were local Bedouins who thought they knew where the nomads would take the women. I suggested we try to find Allesandri but the men said our group were now far to the west and there was no time to spare if we were to catch up with the nomads.

I felt I could trust the men who seemed to know something about me and I followed them as they trotted off towards the east. We continued until nightfall without any communication or stopping to rest whereupon we camped under the stars but with no fire I found it too cold to sleep.

The men could speak Arabic although this was not their native tongue they also knew Allesandri and were grateful for the corsair's help in the past. It seemed they knew the likely route the nomads would take back to their homes in the interior although not their final destination which, where nomads were concerned was, not surprisingly, for ever changing.

We shared the food we had but limited ourselves as the duration of our journey could not be defined and it may be our provisions which would determine our tracking time. It was still dark when we set off in the direction the Bedouins felt we would cut across the nomad's tracks, although at the pace we set I hoped we would not miss the signs. I need not have worried as these men, who introduced themselves as Zayed and Abduallah, were obviously expert trackers and after about three hours they stopped and after jumping down from their horses showed us where some animal spoor was intermingled with that of horses and camels.

'The nomads have come across a small herd of sable antelope and they have obviously followed their trail looking for food.'

'Let us hope their greed, or their need for food will slow them down,' said Zayhed.

We all agreed this could be the mistake we were looking for, as the Bedouins had intimated we might find it difficult to catch up with the nomads before they reached their homeland on the plateau.

My brief experiences of the desert conditions made me realize what a dangerous environment it was with its raging heat during the day, near freezing cold at night and unpredictable sandstorms but what we experienced next was one of the strangest episodes of my life.

We could see the mountains in the distance and I had noticed how dark the sky was above the peaks but these were many miles away and I did not contemplate any dangers from this source. The Bedouins also pointed out the clouds and were obviously somewhat concerned.

It was just a couple of hours later that the danger revealed itself and it was a sight I shall never forget.

We were travelling in line across a low, rocky, yet relatively flat area with a small river cliff being our next destination about a half a mile away. This was a wadi or dried up river bed which probably had seen no water for years; however today was the exception. We all stopped in unison as a strange noise growing steadily louder rumbled towards us. I had no idea what the cause of the noise was but the Bedouins obviously did.

'Ride fast to the cliff,' shouted Abduallah as he stirred his horse into a canter.

My camel was slow to respond but urged on by the Bedouins who stayed with me, we gradually picked up speed and were barrelling along recklessly when the water reached us. The wall of water was only a few inches deep to start with but within moments the two Bedouins had to jump off their horses and cling to the animal's necks as the powerful surge of water containing sticks and other debris hit us. My large camel was swept off its feet but remained upright and I hung on to its reins as it tried to swim towards the river bank. I eventually slid down the side of the camel and desperately tried to swim along with her but we were all swept downstream until the river curved and being on the outside of the bend I suddenly found myself in shallower water. The Bedouins on their lighter horses were finding it difficult to reach the shallow water so I turned my reluctant camel around and went back to help them. Both men managed to cling onto the camels' baggage and the strong animal then towed us all into the shallows. Although the water still flowed rapidly we all managed to wade ashore and finally clamber onto dry land. The twelve foot deep, once dry river bed was now a raging torrent and the Bedouins quickly urged me to move away from the river which they said could burst its banks and flood the surrounding area. Once we were about half a mile away from the river and on slightly higher land we stopped to rest. The Bedouins horses looked completely exhausted while the camel, which had gone up vastly in my affections, just stood calmly chewing the cud. We were now on the side of the river we wanted to be and there was certainly no turning back.

It took about an hour of steady riding before the shock of what we had just been through hit me. I started to shiver and felt physically sick. Abduallah noticed my discomfort as I spewed down the side of the camel and he decided we should rest and eat although Zayed trotted off in search of any evidence of our quarry.

There was little vegetation in this rocky desert but we found a large rock and sheltered from the scorching sun under its overhang and I must have fallen asleep because the sound of Zayed's voice made me suddenly attentive.

Abduallah turned to me and explained in simple Arabic that Zayed had found tracks leading to a small oasis which lies around five miles to the east. Before we set off I asked if we had any sort of plan once we caught up with the nomads.

'We will charge them and slaughter them like the dogs they are,' said Zayed theatrically.

The two Bedouins then looked at each other and burst out laughing.

'No we do not have a plan but we must find them first and assess the situation,' said Abduallah in a very military manner.

'You have to remember effendi we have fought many battles under some excellent commanders in our conflicts with either the Arabs or other Bedouins and Zayed and myself both led men into battle. Together the three of us will decide our action when the time comes.'

The time came earlier than I expected when Zayed put his arm in air for us to stop and remain silent. We climbed off our mounts and tied them to some thorn scrub and followed Zayed who slithered like a snake up the side of the dune in front of us.

Below some two hundred yards away was a tiny oasis which contained no more than twenty palms and a well which was situated in the centre. Two tents sat amongst the trees and there was some movement of people who I could not make out. Their animals were tethered between us and the tents and these comprised of four horses and three camels.

'I believe we are up against four men and I expect the three women probably travelled on the camels and are now in one of the tents, suggested Abduallah.

We slid back down the dune and discussed our options.

'We could wait until dark and try to surprise them,' said Zayed.

'Our main problem is we have no firearms,' added Abduallah.

'I have my bow and maybe I could shorten the odds if we can get close enough,' I quickly added, although as soon as I had, I started to think about what this really entailed.

'We must make sure these are the men we have been following before we act but then we must act quickly,' said Abduallah.

We watched the oasis through a bush which sat on a nearby rocky outcrop and our suspicions were soon proved to be correct as a woman was manhandled out of one of the tents and dragged towards a fire where cooking pots were arranged.

'I recognize the woman,' said Zayed. 'She is definitely from the village.'

Eventually all three women were made to cook for the four men who were lounging under the trees and who had obviously slaughtered a sable which now hung from a tree.

'Now is as good a time as any,' I suggested. 'If you could make a diversion to the south then I could get nearer from behind that large dune to the north. I think I could disable two men and that might make them give up quickly if we can convince them that there are many of us.'

Our plan was agreed upon and we moved into place after a warm embrace from Zayed which quite took me by surprise.

'Whatever is going to happen Solomon we will always be in your debt for saving us from the flood. May your god go with you,' said Abduallah who in turn embraced me, then turned, leapt on his horse and trotted after Zayed who was positioning himself for the ruse to start on my signal.

I flashed a reflection using the back of my silver compass case in the direction of the Bedouins hidden position and the diversion started with the two horsemen dashing backwards and forwards just below the crest of the dune shouting what seemed like orders to others. Even from my position on the other side of the camp it seemed there must be dozens of men on the other side of the dune. I presumed the nomads would be looking away from me so I ran over the top and down the side of my dune until I was only forty yards from the camp.

The nomads were facing away from me with two of them holding long muskets. I shouted at them in Arabic to drop their weapons but one lifted his weapon whereupon I loosed an arrow which caught him in the throat. The second armed man tried to hide behind a tree but before he could fully hide I shot him in the side. Both men were probably mortally wounded and I hoped the shock of the attack would make the other two nomads, only armed with swords, quickly surrender but I was wrong.

Zayed and Abduallah had by now galloped into the camp and were shouting at the Bedouins in their own language. It seemed they were telling the nomads to surrender but at the same time were goading them to fight. My friends then dismounted and faced the nomads who were also pointing to me.

'I have said if they defeat Zayed and myself that you will take the women but not harm these two men. This is a fight of honour and must be fought as such.'

I nodded although I was prepared to down these two if I felt I needed to.

The fight was ferocious but short. The nomads were aggressive, brave opponents but could not match the skill of my Bedouins who first injured then killed the nomads.

We buried the four men and Abduallah and Zayed comforted the women who had not been harmed, but said the men had captured them to be sold as slaves. We then made sure the sable meat did not go to waste and rested before starting back in the morning. During the night we took turns to keep watch, because we realized that the other half of the nomad group could still be at large, but there were no disturbances and we set off at first light.

Abduallah and Zayed were now armed with the nomad's muskets and with the women, their camels and the nomad's horses, we navigated our way back to the meeting place we had arranged earlier. I continued to be amazed at the Bedouins sense of direction but I was pleased with my own efforts which seemed to correlate with theirs.

I had worried about the fate of Luke and Duncan and it was to my great relief that on arriving at the oasis we were greeted by my great friends, the rest of Musabi's group as well as Allesandri and his men. It transpired that the other nomad group was expected to lead us off the scent but they had been caught and captured without loss of life.

These men were now tethered to two palms and closely guarded by Allesandri's men. There was a great feeling of joy in that we had recaptured the women although this was tempered by the sadness at losing two men in the first altercation in the sandstorm. Allesandri explained that the four captured men would be given to the village that had been attacked and that they would decide the punishment.

Chapter Eleven

THE IRISH SLAVE

We arrived at Sale early in the morning to be met by the aromas and smells of spices, burning firewood, sewage and the sea. We passed through narrow winding alleyways past a mosque and many small shops until our route opened up into a white and blue tiled plaza with a bubbling fountain in the centre. It was at one of the houses surrounding the square, that we were greeted by some of Allesandri's friends who agreed to accommodate us. We were asked to camp in the grounds and were then invited to bathe in sumptuous surroundings which were rather embarrassingly attended by some very nubile young women. We dressed and later ate with the owner who was simply known as Sadiq and who laughed uproariously at the tale that led us to be in his company.

'I have heard the men call you The Lion Killer now I know why,' he said.

The next day we went with Allesandri to the slave market, which was an outdoor affair in a sheltered courtyard, attached to the Souk. For the first hour a succession of African men were brought out and sold to the highest bidder and although I felt sympathy for the men my attention was taken by some chatter and arguing behind me. The group were mostly women and the argument seemed to be over one woman who was seated and fully covered by a long hooded white robe.

'What is going on over there Captain?' I asked Allesandri.

He watched for a few moments and then replied that the hooded woman was to be sold and it seems that some of the other women did not want her in their household and are trying to stop their husbands' bidding.

Duncan and Luke had sidled away from the slave area and I saw them entering a nearby building where men were sitting outside drinking but my attention was redirected to the woman on the stool who suddenly stood up and marched herself into the centre of the slave ring. The men who had been bidding or watching the slave auction stopped their chatter and there was an audible gasp as the woman threw off her robe and stood naked in front of the throng.

She then shouted 'I am a Celtic Queen and cannot be enslaved; whoever buys me will be cursed forever and will never produce any sons.'

The crowd reacted strangely with some hurling abuse while others laughed rather weakly.

'I am surprised she has not been bought, raped or executed by now,' said Allesandri.

'You know of this woman Captain?'

'I do indeed Solomon, as it was on one of our raids that she was captured. Murat Rais rarely captures Celts but this one slipped through the net and has been causing problems ever since. A local merchant who could not handle her bought her and I think it is Murat Rais's liking of the Celts that has stopped her being abused or killed. She certainly is a striking figure which is why those women do not want her in their household and you can possibly see their point.'

The woman had now covered herself with her robe but still stood defiantly in the middle of the ring. It was at this point that I did something that would affect at least one of our lives forever.

'How much would a woman like her cost?' I asked.

'Probably three gold pieces, why are you thinking of bidding?' laughed Allesandri. Looking at the expression on my face he added, 'you are aren't you?'

'Could I, if I could afford it?'

'I can't see why not, although if I bid for you it might keep away any possible competition. How much money do you have?'

'Not enough.'

Allesandri thought for a moment and then put forward a proposition.

'I will buy the girl for you but you will have to pay me back by performing a task for me later.'

'What sort of task?'

Seeing my look of consternation Allesandri assured me the task would not break my ethics but that I alone might be able to help him in the future.

'I do not expect to be a corsair forever and I will need friends back in Europe to help me integrate into society. Would you, if you return safely to England, be prepared to welcome me as a friend and not relate my true background?'

'I would try to help if I could although England is not the easiest place for anyone at the moment and could be considerably difficult for an Islamic pirate.'

We both laughed at the thought but I assured the Captain that I would help him if I could.

'That's good enough for me, now let's make a bid.'

There was no competition and two gold pieces secured the trade.

'What happens now?' I asked.

'You sign the traders docket and she is yours to do with as you wish and good luck to you, I think you will need it.'

The money was paid and the document signed before I approached the woman.

'You pirate scum, have you now summoned up the courage to have your way with me after all this time or am I to be resold again because of your fear of me?'

This was not the place to explain matters so I held the woman by her arm and led her away from the crowd who were now more interested in other slaves who would perhaps be rather less trouble.

'Who's this?' said Duncan who bumped into the woman as we passed the inn.

'If you want to know I have just bought a slave,' I said rather testily and a rather bemused Duncan and Luke followed us back to the camp.

'Who is she Solomon and whatever made you buy a slave and how did you pay for her?' rattled out Luke when we reached our tents.

'I am not sure why I bought her, she looked lost despite her aggression and she, like us had been captured by the corsairs. I believe she is from Ireland.'

'I don't suppose her obvious beauty had anything to do with your purchase?' asked Duncan, who was staring at the woman who sat on a tree stump near to our tents.

'Well maybe so, but the fact remains she has suffered the same plight as ourselves and I felt it my duty to try and help her.'

'Good for you Solomon, I applaud your motives,' said Duncan.

'I also applaud your eye for a woman and no mistake,' said a more pragmatic Luke who was also staring at the woman who was now staring back.

'Well have you fine gentlemen decided my fate yet?' she said waspishly.

'I think you should announce your intentions if you know what they are,' said Duncan.

I gave him a hard stare but agreed that I should explain our position to the woman.

'I am Solomon and these are my friends and compatriots Duncan and Luke. May I ask your name?'

Being rather taken aback by the civility of my question she replied calmly.

'My name is Teagan and I come from a village in West Cork in Ireland. Our village was raided and I was taken prisoner. I have been in this hellhole for over six months with seemingly no hope of returning,' she said angrily.

'You said you were a Celtic Queen.'

'My family was highly influential in the area around West Cork and first my mother and then I, was called The Queen of Cork by local people. I thought it might impress the bidders but it seems it made no difference.'

I then explained our situation to Teagan whose attitude changed as she realised we might actually be able to help her.

'You must realise we have no idea when we might leave this place but until then you are in our care and although not our slave it might be better if you keep a low profile while we organise our return.'

With that she burst into tears and hugged Duncan who was the nearest to her before reaching for my and Luke's hand.

'Thank you for your kindness, I will repay you with my loyalty and I will work for you as a maid if needs be.'

'That maybe the best option so it looks as though we have bought you for a reason other than the obvious,' I said blushing.

Luke laughed and clapped me on the shoulder saying: 'You never cease to amaze me Solomon,' before walking back to his tent.

We found a tent for Teagan, which Duncan erected whilst showing a great deal of attention to detail and a fair amount of attention to our new guest. I felt a surprising chemistry had already developed between the two of them in the few moments they had been together.

We had now spent over seven months in Morocco before any chance to return to England materialised. In that time we were beginning to wonder if Murat Rais was really interested in finding us a return berth and although our time spent in Safi was illuminating we all felt we should back in England fighting for our cause. The only major development was the romance between the volcanic Irish Teagan and dour Scotsman Duncan. They now shared a tent and seemed hopelessly in love between bouts of verbal fireworks.

Sam and Joe had integrated into the fishermen's sector and were always on the lookout for possible transport and Luke and I had spent time with the locals doing more hunting, although none of the escapades quite lived up to the excitement of the lion-killing day. We tracked and killed deer for food but also leopard, which we lured into a trap with a tethered goat. The leopard had killed some local goats and we were asked to help find and kill it. Whenever we killed such an animal there seemed to be a huge level of excitement during the hunt followed by a certain level of regret and awe once the deed had been done. Luke said he always felt like that even when killing a rabbit. The only animal he seemed to have little affection for was the fox. We saw a number in the desert and although they seemed to be doing no harm Luke always tried to kill them.

'They are the only animal I know that seems to kill for fun. Get them in a hen house and they will kill them all and take one,' he said shaking his head.

Despite all the interesting facets of our time in Morocco I could see we were all now getting a little irritable which was a sure sign that we had to move on and soon before trouble started.

The worst of all possible news came to us via the captain of one of Murat Rais' raiders who had returned from a foray in the English Channel where he had captured a merchantman from England. The captain of the merchantman had said that King Charles no longer ruled, that his army had been well beaten at a place called Naseby and he was now in hiding, probably in Scotland. Parliamentarians now ruled and supporters of the King were being imprisoned and some executed.

This news brought with it so many unanswered questions and my first thought was for my family and Betsy, although I knew my father and sisters had fled to France.

That evening the six of us met to talk about the news and we all wondered not only how we could get back to England but also what we could expect when we got there. Duncan suggested that Scotland might be the safest place or even Ireland where he had friends and family.

I felt it important that the gravity of this news should be explained to Murat Rais and the next day I sought out Musabi and explained the situation. He said he would approach Murat Rais with our suggestion that Ireland would be a suitable destination.

Chapter Twelve

THE RETURN
(March 1645)

It was another two weeks before we received a reply from Murat Rais and this came in the form of an invitation to dinner, although Teagan was unsurprisingly not included, with Captain Allesandri. The meal was a jolly affair as we had all come to respect and indeed admire the flamboyant Venetian captain despite his piratical deeds.

'Now gentlemen the time has come for me to explain why I have brought you here. We have decided to sail a fleet to Portugal and take revenge on Santos who was the person responsible for the attack on the fleet you were in some months ago. We then intend to go on to Ireland where we have business of a different kind that need not concern you. I am offering you passage to Ireland but of course

I would expect you to be willing to help us take revenge on Santos along the way.

Looking around our group I could see a few shrugs and nods and although no one wanted to make the decision for us all I felt I should make my feelings know.

'I have no liking for Santos who killed two of our men and I for one am keen to get back to England as soon as possible.'

'Murat Rais has said you may stay if you wish but passages to Northern Europe are few and far between and it may be some time before another opportunity arises.'

Duncan and Luke quickly agreed that they would be only too willing to give Santos a bloody nose while Sam and Joe seemed quite animated at the prospect of getting back to soldiering, even if it was as part of a corsair band.

'Excellent, we leave the day after tomorrow and Musabi will help you with the organisation.'

The next day we were busy packing our belongings that included some fine examples of local armoury, which we had all admired. Luke with his scimitar and local clothes certainly looked the part and even his Arabic was now good enough to make simple conversation.

We boarded the Xebec early the next day and were assigned duties before being greeted by Captain Allesandri who reminded us that we were now under his command. Teagan was not the only woman aboard and she was given galley duties and shared their basic accommodation.

It was now March and the baking hot weather of North Africa was left behind as we sailed out into the Atlantic where the cool strong breeze from the west helped us make good speed towards our destination which we had now been told was the island of Madeira. The Captain informed us that Santos had been seen with his fleet heading towards the Portuguese island to the north west and he intended to either tackle him at sea or, if need be, on the island itself. None of us had known the location of the island although we had all heard of or had drunk Madeira wine.

'It is a mountainous island with only one real port and although we have raided the island before, it would not be a simple task and therefore I hope we have a sea encounter where our large force should be far too strong for Santos,' said the captain.

It was indeed a large force with three Xebecs and four Polaccas each containing probably eighty to one hundred men. With powerful guns and well-trained crews this was truly a powerful fleet although I could sense Allesandri's apprehension regarding a land based assault.

During daylight the fleet made swift progress and kept in a surprisingly tight formation whilst at night our speed hardly decreased and each boat was well lit with lanterns to help keep the group together. Captain Allesandri showed Duncan and I where we were on a chart and he explained that we would try to cut off Santos before he reached Funchal the main port on Madeira.

'Time is on Santos' side although the wind has been in our favour. Also by not decreasing our speed at night we may have gained some water. If we are to intercept him it will probably be sometime late tomorrow afternoon when the island should be clearly in view.'

True to his calculations the island of Madeira began to loom up on the horizon around the middle of the following day but it was not until dusk that a sail was sighted towards the north. More shouts from the masthead informed us that indeed there was a fleet of probably four boats heading along an intercept course with us.

'He will see us soon and then he has a choice, either turn and run before the wind and into the night knowing that we will probably catch up with him within six hours if we do not lose sight of him. Or make a dash for Funchal which might be difficult against the westerly now blowing steadily.'

'Which would you choose?' I asked rather naively.

'Well I would hope not to get into that position in the first place,' replied Allesandri rather haughtily, 'but now you ask, I feel he will hope he can outrun us into Funchal.'

The captain was correct as the men aloft reported more sail being applied to the enemy ships, which were now moving in a direct line towards us.

'He will come as close as he dare and then tack back towards Funchal and hope he can out run us. It will be a close call,' said the captain who seemed to like our presence whilst he displayed his considerable sailing skills.

Our whole fleet was now moving at great pace and the thrill of the sleek Xebecs under full sail made me start to appreciate Allesandri's obvious love of sailing. We regularly plummeted down into a trough of one of the large Atlantic swells before crashing into the wave as it started to loom up in front of us. This was no storm but the ocean was alive with a powerful swell and we were riding it under full sail and with an increasingly excitable crew. These men were desperate to take revenge on Santos and cheered as we hammered our way through more waves heading straight for our enemy. When all of his fleet were not more than two miles away, they suddenly turned onto a starboard tack and fled for the safe haven of Funchal.

We certainly were gaining on the fleeing fleet but could we catch them before they reached the harbour, was the question all the sailors must have been thinking because after a short interval of shouting and cheering, the crew became almost silent as we sped on in the wake of Santos.

The four boats ahead seemed to be moving at similar speeds although one, according to Sam, seemed to be sending up even more sail.

'He is risking losing a spar if he puts on too much sail,' he said pointing to the most easterly boat.

Sure enough the captain of this boat must have panicked into trying to get more speed out of his vessel and true to Sam's prediction, there was a sudden tumble of sailcloth and rigging from the topsail and the boat slowed significantly.

Under Allesandri's orders flags were sent aloft and two of our Polaccas veered off in the direction of the doomed vessel where panic seemed to have set in on deck, as men ran around feverishly trying to right the captain's mistake. After thirty minutes the Polaccas were swarming up behind the boat before swerving around the starboard side when cannon fire was exchanged.

'The Polaccas have crossed to the starboard side from where their port cannons can fire easily, look, the other vessel is so low in the water on that side they can hardly make a shot.'

The two Polaccas fired broadsides into the enemy causing massive damage before closing and eventually boarding from both sides. It was a very one sided affair and although we could see many of their sailors were killed and thrown overboard, most were herded below and a prize crew was installed before the Polaccas eventually continued in our wake, although by now some way behind and out of the main race.

Madeira was now a towering mass in front of us and we could see the port in the distance. We had gained on Santos but it seemed unlikely that we would be able to catch and overhaul him before he reached what he must think would be the safety of the harbour. This was a reasonable assumption as we were told there were cannon on the fort walls around the port entrance and covering fire could make life difficult for us if we got too close. However Allesandri had other ideas. He sent messages by flag to the others boats, which were sailing in close order with no more than a few hundred yards between them. Santos was now only half a mile ahead and we could see men waving from the stern of their rearmost vessel as they obviously thought they had won the race and would soon be able to dash into the safety of the harbour. Santos probably expected our fleet to turn away from the port but instead there was a quick flurry of orders and we could see the whole of our fleet suddenly put on extra sail. Our boat lurched forward and keeled over to starboard as we accelerated towards the enemy. The gap closed so quickly that the enemy could not respond before we were almost level with them and amongst them. Shots were fired by most boats but it seemed the race was more important than the fight and to my surprise, no shots were fired from the fortifications.

'We are too close together for the fort to be able to pick out a clear target,' said Sam. 'It looks as though we are going straight into the lion's den right on the lion's tail.'

He was right; we followed the enemy boats at breakneck speed into the harbour before swinging round into the wind.

'Fire,' shouted Allesandri and our broadside crashed into the boat only a few yards away.

What happened next in the harbour is difficult to say and afterwards there were a number of different versions told and retold over a glass or two. There was mayhem aboard our boat as we crashed into the side of an enemy vessel, and our obvious focus was to gain control of our nearest foe. We boarded shouting and screaming with the rest of the crew and after an initial burst of muskets and pistols from both sides, it was down to hand-to-hand fighting. Luke, Duncan and I managed to clamber aboard the low quarterdeck of the enemy and were immediately set upon by a horde of Santos' men. Fighting next to Duncan is an education in how to kill quickly and Luke and I had now had enough exposure to his methods to be able to fight in a similar way. He simply bullies his enemy by fast rapid blows of his sword while using a short sword in his left hand to maim and dispatch his confused opposition. With all three of us confronting the horde in the same way they suddenly stopped and by backing off they got in each other's way. Their attack completely lost momentum whereupon we charged into them and cut them down before the ones at the rear ran back down the steps to the main deck, where they ran into a mass of our men who by now had virtually secured the ship.

It was at this point we were able to look around to see what the overall position was and it soon became obvious that our fleet had overwhelmed Santos' men and the sailors were now quickly dividing their time between persecuting the enemy and securing the boats in the harbour.

We clambered back onto Allesandri's boat where we were greeted with laughs and slaps on the back as the Captain issued orders regarding the prisoners.

'What about the fort?' I asked.

'I doubt if there will be many people around ashore when we land. We have been here before and the locals make for the hills when an attack is imminent and I doubt if anyone will be manning anything other than a donkey.'

We spent four days on Madeira and as the Captain had surmised there were no locals to be found and much looting and drinking seemed to be the main object for most of the men, and although drinking alcohol was frowned upon in Morocco, once the men were abroad these transgressions seemed to be ignored. The Captain made sure the prisoners were well guarded and lookouts posted but most of the men had the run of the town and came back with sacks of loot and even barrels of wine.

Santos was captured alive and kept in the hold of our boat until the second day when he and eight of his lieutenants were summarily executed on the beach and their severed heads posted on pikes along the fort walls. These corsairs again displayed their completely bipolar attitude. If you are with them they are loyal and gregarious, against them and their barbarism shows no bounds.

'I see you have not helped yourselves to the riches of Madeira,' said the Captain on the second afternoon of our stay. 'I can understand your reluctance to become fully-fledged corsairs but I do believe you should share in the spoils of our conquest.

We have not yet fully investigated Santos' vessel, you therefore have my permission to take whatever you wish for yourselves before I allow my men to remove any remaining riches.'

'Well I for one would be pleased to relieve Santos of his chattels as he has already killed two of us and he won't have much use for riches where he has gone,' said Duncan.

We agreed and the five of us were ferried across the bay to where Santos' flagship was moored. Similar to a Polacca his boat was well armed and despite the damage done we could easily move around the cabins and lower deck. There were a few trinkets lying around in the rubble of the partly destroyed cabin and we gathered them up to be shared out later. Duncan pushed over the captain's desk and found a loose board underneath where he discovered a sack of more silver cups and some silver coins. On further investigation another two small hordes of silver were found before we found the real treasure.

Behind the captain's cot the panelled wall looked unusually unscratched or damaged and I picking up a discarded musket and stove in the wall with the butt of the weapon whereupon a shower of gold coins came flooding out onto the deck. We all stared in astonishment before collecting them up carefully and stowing them in three separate leather satchels we found in a locker. We also removed the captain's chest, which we thought might come in useful at a later date.

As the various corsairs returned to the flagship it was clear that they had all found riches of one sort or another and therefore showed little interest in what we had found. We stowed our loot in the chest amongst our belongings and used the lock we had found with it to secure it, with Duncan keeping the key. We were to leave Madeira the next day so before we left, Luke and I decided to go ashore and explore the Island.

Funchal was a small town but seemingly flourishing due to its wine trade. There also seemed an ingenious system of small canals called levadas, which lead down from the mountains by running along the contours of the slopes and distributing water to the vineyards and small farms. We followed one of these levadas and then after a couple of hours sat down to take in the view of the harbour and the coastline. The rugged and spectacular view however could not break my thoughts of home.

It's a grand view but not much like Oxfordshire is it?' said Luke, who had again guessed my thoughts.

'We must get home as soon as we can Luke but I am fearful of what we might find. I am not even sure how we are going to be received when we land in England.'

'We can only take things as we find them, no use worrying about the unknown,' said the pragmatic Luke.

'You are right, shall we climb further?'

'Might as well I feel I need to stretch my legs on dry land after all this splashing about on water.'

After a short while we came across a track leading into the woodland, which had obviously been used recently and we both stood still casting around for any movements. We did not hear a sound which is why Luke dived on top of me just as a musket ball slapped into the tree beside us. We rolled into the nearby levada, which had about a foot of water in it and scurried back in the direction from which we had come before summoning up the courage to peer over the edge of the canal.

'There, in that gap,' said Luke pointing to a space in the trees. 'Two of them, running back up the hill. I think we should get back down before anybody else turns up.'

Now that would have been the sensible thing to do but we were both curious about where the locals were hiding and decided to climb the hill vertically and see what was over the other side. The slope was steep and we travelled quietly and carefully until we reached the summit. We crept along the top until we were suddenly given a clear view of a valley below. It was like a hidden world. Completely surrounded by woodland, mountain slopes and ravine-like valleys, this place must be the hideout for the people of Funchal. Below we could see fields, huts and even what looked like a church. After a few minutes of amazement we both decided now was certainly the time to return, which we did with thankfully no more excitement.

'I think we will keep that piece of knowledge to ourselves Luke, the corsairs have taken enough from this place.'

Luke nodded and we never spoke of the hidden valley with the church again.

The journey from Madeira to Ireland was fairly uneventful but nonetheless exhilarating and illuminating. I was beginning to enjoy life at sea and when I had the opportunity I practiced the art of navigation with some tuition from the Captain and also Sam. The rigging was intricate but in essence straightforward and I was allowed regular turns at the wheel, where I started to feel the connection between wind and sail.

The coast of Ireland loomed up after only five days sailing as the fair westerly aided our voyage. It had been decided to set us down during the hours of darkness in west Cork, whereupon the fleet would carry on to their undisclosed destination.

Captain Allesandri approached me during the final afternoon and asked me to meet with him in his cabin.

'I have kept my side of the bargain Solomon now I wish to explain your side. I will be leaving the fleet in Scotland and eventually I will travel south to London where I hope to exchange some of my property. I have a merchant ship within my fleet and I will approach England as an Italian trader. I will need someone to vouch for me at some time and that is where you come in. I expect you to keep me informed as to your whereabouts through a network of inns which we corsairs have established in your country. At the appropriate time I will call for your assistance and I would be grateful if you could agree to this.'

'I will keep my promise although I am not sure how useful my name will be after what has happened.'

'I am willing to take the risk that your family name will still be an honourable one even after the war, now go and prepare yourself for your final voyage and I wish you luck.'

With that we parted, once enemies now friends and confidants. Later that night the six of us were rowed ashore to a point known by Teagan as being safe but isolated.

Teagan assured us that we should aim to visit her village where we would be welcomed and assisted in our future ventures. The village was about three miles from our landing point and we reached it in the early hours of the morning. The track from the beach to the village passed through a wood and Duncan suggested we wait until early morning before surprising the settlement with the return of their 'Queen.'

At dawn Duncan escorted Teagan to the village while we watched from the edge of the wood. They immediately called at a hut and even at our distance away from the scene we could hear the wails of delight from the people greeting Teagan. After a short while most of the village was gathered out in the area between the huts and Duncan waved for us to go down and join them.

A tall handsome flame haired woman, who surely must be Teagan's mother, greeted us tearfully and other members of the village soon swarmed around us trying to find out how their beautiful relative had so unexpectedly returned. The day and the night was taken up with a major celebration and much food and drink was consumed before we all retired exhausted, but joyous in the knowledge we had at least returned one of the captured members of the village.

It was the following day when decisions had to be made about our next steps and the six of us sat in a circle discussing the options.

'Teagan and I wish to stay together,' was the fairly unsurprising news from Duncan, 'but until we know the situation in England then I feel she should stay here until things become more settled.'

I didn't think this would go down too well and sure enough Teagan exploded, as only she can, and basically told Duncan what he could do with his idea and she was in fact going wherever he did.

To this day I have never met anyone except Teagan who could control Duncan in this way and he soon backed down agreeing that she should accompany him to Scotland at least.

We all decided to go to Scotland and then to England once we had found out more about the political situation.

It took us a week to reach Scotland and another week to find out enough information for us to realise that we would probably not be welcome in England. King Charles was somewhere in Scotland and there were rumours of him gathering an army to reclaim his throne. Following this information Duncan, Sam and Joe decided to wait north of the border so that they could join the King's forces. I however decided to go back to Oxfordshire and Luke was only too keen to do likewise. We sadly parted company with our friends after a year of tackling adventures together and we all hoped we could join forces again in the future.

Our treasure was evenly split once a small portion was given to Teagan. This small portion was large enough for her to become one of the wealthiest local people and she wept with delight and surprise when we presented her with her allocation. Individually our portions made us seriously rich men and Luke I decided to leave a large portion of riches with a reputable moneylender who was used to dealing with gold. Although we were apprehensive Duncan felt sure our money would be safe as these newly developing financial establishments depended on trust without which they would gain no business.

Travelling south was easier than we thought and as we were careful we encountered no real problems. It seemed there was a lull in the condemnation of the King's followers and we arrived in Oxford to find that my family home had been confiscated, my father and sisters were still in France and my two brothers were thought to be alive and probably in Scotland.

Sitting in my room in the inn late at night, waiting for Luke to return from a fact-finding excursion, I heard a series of noises below, which ended in a loud crash. I could see nothing from the window so sword in hand I rushed down and after unbolting the back door I looked out into the courtyard. By now everything was quiet until a body appeared from behind some barrels and staggered towards me. I raised my weapon only to suddenly realise that it was Luke who fell into my arms. I dragged him inside and lay him on the floor and after lighting one of the lanterns I could see he had been badly beaten. The innkeeper and his family had by now all been awoken by the activity and began helping me carry Luke upstairs where we laid him on his bed. Luke was now conscious but obviously in pain.

'I think my ribs are broken,' he croaked as he spat blood into a cloth I had picked up to clean his wounds.

Luke did not seem to have any other broken bones but he had obviously taken a severe beating. When he had recovered a little I asked him what had happened.

'I will tell you later,' he said indicating this was news for my ears only.

The innkeeper's family helped to clean his wounds and dress his injuries before retiring with our thanks whereupon Luke explained how he had come to be in such a state.

'I had been around your estate asking what had happened to my family and it seems my father and mother have died of a pestilence, my sister has married a local farmer and my brothers survived Naseby and are probably in Scotland.'

'I am so sorry Luke, your father was a great man who taught me much and you know I loved your mother who really treated me as a son.'

After a few moments I asked Luke how he came to be in a fight.

'Hardly a fight,' he said,' more of an ambush. I was walking back when I was jumped upon by three men who hit me with clubs before kicking me in the ribs. I initially thought these must be highwaymen but they took nothing from me but left me with a message for you. Caxton wants to see you at Archery Field tomorrow at dawn. He said if you do not come he would spread the news of you being a coward and a Royalist.'

'So he rears his head again. Well it's about time we put an end to this. Every time he crops up he injures a friend of mine, now he will have to answer to me.'

After a couple of hours sleep I awoke to find Luke dressed and standing by the window.

'You will need a Second to look after you,' he said and I did not attempt to argue.

We trudged slowly along the lane, which lead to the nearby Archery Field where I had first met Caxton.

'He has never forgiven you for making him look a fool all that time ago Solomon. This is a man full of hate so watch him carefully and he is hardly known for his trustworthiness,' Luke chuckled.

The three of them stood on the top of the hill and they were silhouetted against the hazy rising sun as we climbed the slope towards them.

'So you decided to come then,' said Caxton in a rather overly laidback manner.

'What's this all about Caxton, can't your cronies see you for the coward you are, always hiding behind their fists.'

'This is about revenge Hawke. You have tried to make a fool of me every time our paths have crossed; well this is where it ends. I have chosen pistols, any objection or are you scared to fire a gun?'

'Pistols are fine,' I said rather less confidently than I hoped.

The two pistols were laid on a blanket and the two seconds inspected, loaded and handed them to the protagonists.

'Ten paces then turn and fire,' were the instructions from the third man.

Caxton and I stood back to back and walked the ten paces counted out by the third man. I turned to see Caxton who already in the firing position pressed the trigger of his pistol only to hear a loud 'click' instead of the deadly retort I was expecting. He had violated the code and I tossed my pistol away with a mixture of relief and disgust. Caxton obviously engulfed with rage ran to where his blade was leaning against a tree. He instantly unsheathed the weapon and attacked me without warning. His first slash was wild but furious and I leapt to the side, although not quickly enough to prevent the razor like edge slicing me across my shoulder. I fell on my face and as I turned over Caxton was looming over me ready to bring down his blade when a resounding 'crack' was immediately followed by a neat black hole appearing in Caxton's forehead. He stopped in his tracks, fell to his knees and with a baleful stare on his face fell face first in the dirt.

'Not so fast,' I heard Luke shout.

He stood there with two pistols aimed at Caxton's followers who were in the process of drawing their swords.

'I suggest you take your master and bury him deep. If I ever see either of you again I will kill you.'

We waited for Caxton's men to load their master across his horse's back and ride off before we worked our way back to the inn. Luke had looked at my wound, which was painful, but now not bleeding much and the rather startled innkeeper's wife stitched and dressed the wound.

There was little to keep us in Oxfordshire and so we went in search of Betsy.

On reaching Bristol we went straight for the inn owned by Betsy only to find that she had sold up and according to the new owner was emigrating to America. We caught up with her at an address given to us by the new owner of the inn and the meeting was highly emotional. Betsy cried, I cried and even Luke had a tear in his eye although he would not admit it. We outlined our tale, which Luke embellished by explaining why Caxton's shot had missed its target.

'It's amazing what a little grease in the wrong place can achieve. I knew he would do something underhand and I was not taking any chances,' he said. Luke's ingenuity had again saved my life.

Betsy then explained why she was moving to America.

'If you remember I was born out of wedlock and my father was a wealthy man who had his English lands confiscated. However, I have a friend who is a lawyer and he has managed to regain some of my father's land. The problem is its location: America. It transpires that my father owned considerable land and farms in Virginia and surprisingly he left these to me in his will and these are now legally mine. I have decided to go and find out what the situation is; do you want to come with me?'

The question came out of the blue but Luke and I could see little future for us in England at the present time and with little hesitation agreed to adventure forth to North America.

The unpredictable future in England must have dawned on others at about the same time as unexpected visitors who arrived a few weeks later buoyed our spirits and made me realise the responsibility I had towards my friends.

Betsy and I were residing in a rented accommodation close to the port in Bristol and were busy discussing the purchase of a suitable craft when our servant announced some visitors.

The look on my face and my speechless welcome brought some ribald comments from Duncan who entered the room followed by Teagan, Sam and Joe.

'What happened in Scotland?' I eventually asked.

'The King has failed to raise an army and as you probably know he has now been arrested. The immediate future for us all is bleak so we decided to seek you out.'

Duncan's explanation for the reason for their arrival was immediately followed by me offering them an alternative.

'Betsy and I are in the process of buying a boat and we intend to travel to America where Betsy has inherited some land. We do not know what to expect but while the situation here is so unsettled we feel this is the right thing to do. We would be honoured to have you all with us if you wish to join us in this adventure.'

That evening was a joyous meeting of what seemed more like a family rather than just friends and in the morning Duncan pronounced that they had all decided enthusiastically to join us on our voyage.

After finding a suitable vessel, captain and crew we left messages for our families and Captain Allesandri as to our whereabouts and circumstances, which we did in various, already agreed, locations.

Four weeks later I sailed with my new bride Betsy and my five friends with our fortunes stowed below and the prospects of an exciting future stretching before us.

On the second day of the voyage Luke presented me with a letter.

'It's from your brother Tom, it was left with the harbour master who put it with the Captains correspondence. He has only just come across it and asked me to give it to you.'

I was excited about the possibility of hearing the news about my family which when I read the letter was encouraging with everyone safe in France. However the main reason for the letter was made obvious when he wrote:

'Dear Solomon,

I have recently been informed of some news I knew I should send to you as soon as possible. Rebecca and her family are safe and well. The storm which affected their boat eventually beached in Spain and after some months of negotiations the family and crew were able to return to France. Rebecca has fully recovered from her ordeal. I found out about your marriage of which Rebecca is aware.

The rest of the family including Ben are safe in France and I am off to Ireland to see what support can be drummed up to help the King.

I wish you well on your adventure to America.

Your loving brother.

Tom.'

* * *

THE END OF BOOK 1

Follow the adventures of Solomon and friends in North America in Book 2

Historical Note

It was a period of time, which first divided and then changed the politics, society, religion and monarchy in Britain forever.

Characters such as Prince Rupert, Lord Fairfax and Oliver Cromwell were all major figures of the time and Solomon follows a route which coincides with some of the major troop movements of the day.

The Siege of Latham and the other battles occurred as stated with a little writer's licence.

It was also a time, which provoked differences of opinion between social groups, countries, counties and even families.

It was a time of choosing sides, violence and treachery. It was a time like no other.

Jan Janszoon was a renowned Barbary Corsair who originated from The Netherlands. He was captured by pirates but eventually became a great leader and Governor of part of Morocco. He was named Murat Rais after converting to Islam as was required by all the Corsairs, some of whom partook in raids on Western Ireland and spent some time on the Isle of Lundy from where they raided the Devon and Cornish coasts.

On Madeira the Nun's Valley is known through local legend as the hidden valley where residents of Funchal retreated to when they were under threat from Corsairs.

Appendix

*Janissaries were soldiers, originally of the Turkish Ottoman Empire. At first they may have been recruited from war prisoners. Later, they were recruited by systematic abduction of Christian youths from their families into the devshirmeh system, which raised them as soldiers from a young age (as young as 8 but as old as 20) in special academies. They were forced to convert to Islam, as non-Muslims were not allowed to bear arms.

*Polacca—a well armed, three-masted fast but small boat popular with pirates.

*Xebec—A large ship with three lanteen-rigged masts. Fast and well armed.